"I won't stop you building the runway."

Cindy took a shaky breath and met Jake's eyes. "I'd made up my mind before the near crash, although I don't suppose you'll believe that."

"I know you do change your mind."

Summoning her reserves, she faced him steadily. "Yes, I *did* change my mind the night you tried to seduce me. I got carried away...but not enough to forget what you really wanted from me."

"Surely you didn't think—"

"And as for the runway," she went on, determined to say her piece. "You thought it was selfishness that made me refuse your request. Well, maybe it was. But not in the way you think."

Cindy loved Jake—in a way she hadn't loved her husband. Which made what had happened before his death infinitely worse!

WELCOME
TO THE WONDERFUL WORLD
OF *Harlequin Romances*

Interesting, informative and entertaining,
each Harlequin Romance portrays an appealing
and original love story. With a varied array
of settings, we may lure you on an African safari,
to a quaint Welsh village, or an exotic Riviera
location—anywhere and everywhere that adventurous
men and women fall in love.

As publishers of Harlequin Romances, we're
extremely proud of our books. Since 1949,
Harlequin Enterprises has built its publishing
reputation on the solid base of quality and
originality. Our stories are the most popular
paperback romances sold in North America; every
month, six new titles are released and sold at
nearly every book-selling store in Canada and the
United States.

For a list of all titles currently available,
send your name and address to:

HARLEQUIN READER SERVICE,
(In the U.S.) P.O. Box 52040, Phoenix, AZ 85072-2040
(In Canada) P.O. Box 2800, Postal Station A
5170 Yonge Street, Willowdale, Ont.   M2N 6J3

We sincerely hope you enjoy reading
this Harlequin Romance.

Yours truly,

THE PUBLISHERS
Harlequin Romances

Lord of the Air

Carol Gregor

Harlequin Books

TORONTO • NEW YORK • LONDON
AMSTERDAM • PARIS • SYDNEY • HAMBURG
STOCKHOLM • ATHENS • TOKYO • MILAN

Original hardcover edition published in 1985
by Mills & Boon Limited

ISBN 0-373-02732-X

Harlequin Romance first edition December 1985

Copyright © 1985 by Carol Gregor.
Philippine copyright 1985. Australian copyright 1985.

All rights reserved. Except for use in any review, the reproduction or utilization
of this work in whole or in part in any form by any electronic, mechanical
or other means, now known or hereafter invented, including xerography,
photocopying and recording, or in any information storage or retrieval system,
is forbidden without the permission of the publisher, Harlequin Enterprises
Limited, 225 Duncan Mill Road, Don Mills, Ontario, Canada M3B 3K9. All the
characters in this book have no existence outside the imagination of the
author and have no relation whatsoever to anyone bearing the same name
or names. They are not even distantly inspired by any individual known
or unknown to the author, and all the incidents are pure invention.

The Harlequin trademarks, consisting of the words HARLEQUIN ROMANCE
and the portrayal of a Harlequin, are trademarks of Harlequin Enterprises
Limited; the portrayal of a Harlequin is registered in the United States Patent
and Trademark Office and in the Canada Trade Marks Office.

Printed in U.S.A.

CHAPTER ONE

'MISS Passmore?'

'No,' said Cindy. 'Mrs. Mrs Passmore.'

The stranger was far too big for her low cottage doorway and a spray of the old-fashioned pink rambler which grew around the porch had hooked itself into his thick dark hair. Almost like a guard dog, she thought to herself, and then wanted to laugh at the absurd idea that the roses would protect her from unknown visitors.

But she couldn't imagine who he was, or why he had come. As yet she knew no one in the village. So she kept her face straight, her defences up.

'I'm sorry,' said the stranger. 'I was told——' He shrugged slightly, as if it didn't matter.

She could guess full well what he would have been told. That there was someone new in old Mrs Granger's Rose Cottage. That she was just a young slip of a thing. And that she seemed to be there alone.

She tipped her head to one side, questioning. Her artist's eye took in the impression of a big man, solid but not heavy. But she could not place him. He obviously wasn't an insurance agent, or a milkman. He wore olive green cord trousers pushed down into calf-length leather boots, and a well worn leather jacket with a fringe of sheepskin lining showing where it lay open over a khaki shirt. They were casual, rather strange clothes but they went well with the man's tanned and slightly battered features. An air of quiet command hung about him. He was a man who did not need smart clothes to have presence, she thought. He took it as of right.

'There is something I have to ask you, Mrs Passmore. May I come in?'

The voice was dark and authoritative, with a hint of something she could not put her finger on.

5

'Of course.'

The door, as she pulled it further open, scraped loudly on the uncarpeted floor. She grimaced privately. It must have dropped on its hinges, and would need rehanging, or planing along the bottom. Yet another job to add to the long list already tacked on the kitchen wall! She would be busy till the next century!

'You'll have to ignore the mess. I've only just moved in and I haven't even unpacked properly, I'm afraid.' She walked ahead, into the living room, and indicated the lone chair. 'Most of the furniture is in the barn—until I've finished decorating. But please sit down.'

'No, don't worry. I won't take up much of your time.'

The man's head almost touched the low-beamed ceiling. She had to tilt her chin to look up at him. He gave her a dark, level glance, frankly taking in her slight, curvy form in its tight jeans and T-shirt. In the dim light from the diamond-paned windows her hair gleamed with auburn fire, and she felt the same fire rising in her cheeks under his scrutiny. Then his eyes went round the room, taking in the piled crates, the folded curtains, the paints and brushes.

'Are you here alone? There's work for an army here——'

'Everything's under control.' Almost automatically her chin lifted. He glanced back at her, surprised at the tone in her voice. Then he went to the window and bent to look out across the tangled garden. After a long moment he turned to face her, his hands thrust deep into his jacket pockets.

'I wasn't prying, I can assure you. It's none of my business. But I wanted to be certain I was talking to the right person. You *are* the new owner of Rose Cottage?'

She nodded, watchful.

'All right, let me come to the point. My name is Jake Seaton. I run a flying club up at Haldrome Aerodrome, just across the fields there. I don't know how well you know the area, but it's just off Furrowdale Lane . . .'

'I'm sorry, but I only know the village, and the route to the station.'

'You're from London, then?'

'I was living there,' she acknowledged coolly. She did not know what he wanted, and over the past few years defensiveness had become second nature.

He looked at her, then smiled rather grimly. His jaw was stubborn, she noticed, and there was steel behind his gypsy good looks.

'Mrs Passmore,' he observed, 'in these parts questions like that are considered simply neighbourly. You'll just have to get used to people wanting to know a bit about yourself. It's just normal human curiosity.' He turned back to the window. 'Now if you come over here, you can just see the end of one of the hangars, a couple of fields away beyond your orchard.'

His remark had stung her. She felt reproved, like a schoolgirl. But she wouldn't let him see that. Mutely she stepped across and stood next to him at the window.

'You see—There——' He pointed, but she could see nothing.

'Stand on tip toe. Now then, you see that twisted apple tree on the left? Past there, beyond the field they've just harvested, you can just see a grey roof.'

He pointed again, his arm so close to her cheek that she could smell the leather of his jacket. Again she shook her head.

'Well then, here.' Without warning he circled her shoulders with his other arm and pulled her close against him so that she could share his line of vision. His voice at her ear was deep and firmly instructive.

'Have you got that apple tree? Good. Now follow the line of the branch. You see where it crosses the hedge? Then look straight up the field, past that clump of poppies, directly over the next hedge and its there. Just to the right of those trees on the skyline.'

She followed his directions, she had no choice. But for some reason his hand on her bare elbow felt electric, and his presence behind her made her quiver in his lightly functional embrace.

'Got it now?'

'Yes—yes——'

Rapidly she pulled away from him, her breath uneven. From the look he gave her she knew he had sensed her distress.

'I can see it—but I don't see what it's got to do with me.'

'It's like this, Mrs Passmore. We spend most of our time at that airfield teaching beginners how to fly. At present we've got just the one runway, which is fine when the wind is from the east or west. But when it's from the north or south it can be very tricky taking off and landing. I won't get too technical, but ideally aircraft need the wind directly in front of them, or behind them. I'm sure you can imagine that a wind at ninety degrees to the left or right isn't that healthy, especially if it's strong or gusting. Of course, it's not too bad for experienced pilots, but new students need all their concentration for handling just the basics, without having to worry about dangerous crosswinds. I want to make things as safe as possible for them. For a long time now I've been wanting to build a new runway, lining up north to south. The only trouble is that will mean aeroplanes taking off and landing over your orchard, and noise abatement regulations are pretty strict around here. I need to get planning permission for this work, and that permission depends on you saying you don't mind. Yours is the only house under the flight path, but if you object, my hands are completely tied.'

Cindy looked at Jake Seaton powerful and dark, in the dusty room.

Her room! *Her* cottage!

In the whole twenty-four years of her life no one had ever asked her permission for anything. Before Rose Cottage she had barely had anything to call her own. And Simon had always been very much in charge during their brief marriage.

She swallowed. It was quite a responsibility. Jake Seaton's eyes never left her face, and that somehow made it harder to think clearly. She frowned. He saw the look.

'It wouldn't be like living near Heathrow,' he said. 'We'd probably only use that runway about a third to a quarter of the time, and the aeroplanes are only little things. They wouldn't go over your house, only over your apple trees, and by then they'd be at a good six hundred feet. You'd probably only notice them on take off. On landing they'd be coming in with low power and hardly any noise.'

'Well, Mr Seaton——'

'Jake, please.'

'Well——' she could not use his name, it seemed oddly intimate, '—I don't see why not, if it would help you——' After all, she had a whole two acres to herself. 'But why didn't you ask my aunt?'

'If you mean Mrs Granger, I did. Frequently. But the old lady was adamant. She threatened to report me to the council every time an aircraft put as much as a wingtip over her property—and that could have meant an end to all my operating licences.'

Anger in his voice gave it a harsher timbre, and she suddenly identified the traces of a distant New Zealand accent. Judging by his confident manner, he had knocked about the world a fair bit before ending up in this remote corner of eastern England. But what he was saying concerned her far, far more than his personal history.

She stared at him with wide, anxious eyes. 'You mean my aunt was positively opposed to what you propose?'

'You could say that,' he said grimly. 'I'd be inclined to put it rather more bluntly.'

She clenched her hands and stared down at the floorboards by her feet. Everything was suddenly changed—but how could she tell him? Nails were missing from almost all the boards, she noticed abstractedly, and two or three were rotten and splintered. More work.

Then she forced herself to meet his eyes. 'Then I'm sorry Mr—I'm sorry, but I will have to say no as well. I didn't realise, when you explained the situation, that my aunt had been consulted.'

Without realising it, she held her breath, knowing something unpleasant must come.

'What?'

The word was spat out from contemptuous lips. He stepped towards her. 'Don't you understand what I'm saying? There are people's lives in danger—in quite unnecessary danger because of an old lady's whim. That old lady is dead now, but you intend to keep things just as they are!'

His anger frightened her, but she had to hold her ground. 'I am fully aware that my aunt is dead,' she said icily. 'And yes, I intend to keep things as they are.'

He dashed a hand through his hair and his eyes blackened with impatient scorn. 'It's unbelievable! I can hardly believe my ears! My students would barely ever disturb your tranquil little life! There's no night flying at the field, and it's quiet there all through the week. Yet you would deny other people greater safety in order to preserve every last inch of your own ease and comfort down here on the ground!'

He stode angrily towards the floor.

'No. Please!' She reached out a hand as if to stop him. It wasn't like that. She had to make him understand. But if her aunt had said no——

'I'm sorry, I really am. But it's not up to me.'

He turned in the doorway and his face changed. 'Oh I see—I should be talking to your husband.'

'What? Oh no. That's not it. He's—he's not here. There's only me. But——' It would sound so silly, if she explained it to a stranger.

'But what?' His face hardened again, and he looked back at her with unhidden contempt. 'Haven't you got enough privacy with your mere two acres, or are you frightened of having your afternoon nap disturbed? I hear you're a lady of leisure, Mrs Passmore, so I suppose you'll be following your aunt's example and be spending half your life at the window with binoculars, ready to take down the registration number of any innocent pilot who dares to stray within sight. Well some of us have rather better things to do with our time, so if you'll excuse me——'

The door was shut with a restrained bang. Then the front door shut firmly. She heard steps go down the front path and shortly afterwards the deep roar of a powerful engine accelerated up the lane towards the village. Then there was just a terrible lonely quiet, and the room around seemed chill and cheerless.

Too shocked even to feel outraged at the injustice of his remarks, she sank on to the nearest packing case. Mellow autumn sunlight filtered through the dusty glass to make patterns on the bare floor, but did not penetrate to where she sat in shadow, hugging her elbows.

So that was how she now seemed from the outside! A lady of property and leisure, too concerned with her own comfort to care for others! It was horrible—and it was deeply ironic considering what her life had been like for the past two years.

Not that Jake Seaton would know anything about that. But when she had opened the solicitor's letter and read the overwhelming news that Aunt Beth had bequeathed her Rose Cottage, it had come like a blessed flood of warmth after a long dark winter. She had run downstairs, to the bedsitter beneath hers, and told Sarah the good news. And her friend had hugged her warmly, and told her that if anyone deserved a lucky break she did, and the two of them had toasted dear Aunt Beth in Sarah's last remaining inch of Christmas sherry.

Cindy found herself absurdly near to tears. She had hardly been able to wait to leave London, to leave her shabby bedsitter and her drawing lessons for spoilt rich children and her part-time job at the art gallery. Life had been a constant struggle to make ends meet, and there had never been time for any serious work of her own.

Not that she minded that so much. When she did venture out with her sketch book and set herself to work, crowds quickly gathered to breathe down her neck and jostle her elbow. Shy by nature, she hated to attract that attention.

But she would miss having Sarah downstairs, ever ready with coffee and sympathy. Still, Sarah had said she would come up for a weekend, just as soon as Cindy was settled, and Cindy resolved to make that as soon as possible. Because Jake Seaton's visit had been deeply unsettling, and she longed to explain to someone how things really were.

Aunt Beth's will, written in her own quavery writing, had been quite explicit. 'And Rose Cottage to my grandniece Cindy Granger, now Mrs Cindy Passmore, to keep and preserve as a haven of tranquillity in an increasingly noisome world.' Then the little note, left specially for her. 'Cindy, my dear, Rose Cottage is for you because you need it so badly. Treasure it, and keep it as I would have liked. Not a museum, my dear, but a place of happiness and security. Be happy there, as I was.'

She sighed and looked around. Aunt Beth had been well into her nineties when she died, and in failing mind and health for a long time. Many essential repairs had been neglected. From the small legacy that came with the cottage Cindy had managed to have the roof rethatched, the damp treated, the kitchen and bathroom modernised and the chimneys swept. But there was still a mountain of work to do.

Then the phone rang.

'Hi Cindy, how's it going?'

'Oh Sarah, how lovely to hear your voice! I was just on the point of being defeated by it all.'

'That's what I suspected. So how about me coming down at the weekend and giving you a hand? I can bring a sleeping bag, and a couple of cans of soup.'

Cindy laughed. 'No need. I'll have finished the bedrooms by then. And we *do* have food shops down here. It isn't exactly the last outpost of civilisation.' Her voice was light with gaiety and relief. Sarah's robust good humour would banish Jake Seaton's glowering ghost from the room. Then she thought of something. 'What about Paul? You know he's welcome.' Paul was Sarah's fiancé. They both taught at the same London comprehensive school. She bit her lip. Paul was a love, and he and Sarah were always careful not to make her feel left out. But even so, three was never an easy number.

So it was a relief to hear Sarah say, 'No. He'd love to come and see Ye Olde Ruine, but he's taking some of the third years off canoeing in Wales. So it'll just be little old me, dressed in my best dungarees and clutching a paintbrush!'

'Little old you is more than enough. Forget the paintbrush!'

'Well, we'll see. I'll be there about eight. 'Bye love, take care.'

It was marvellous how the call had lifted her spirits. She wandered out to the kitchen and trailed a hand wonderingly along the glowing wood surfaces of the new kitchen units. A woman of property. She grimaced, then firmly pushed away the memory of Jake Seaton's contempt. He had got it all wrong, but he was nothing to her. Nothing at all.

She opened the back door with a struggle—yet another job to be tackled—and waded out into the overgrown garden flooded with low September sun. Yellow roses were climbing the mellow stonework of the cottage while in the orchard, beyond the arch of honeysuckle, apples were hanging, full and golden on the trees.

She breathed deeply, relishing the clear calm of the late afternoon. Tomorrow she would gather the windfall apples. She would finish wallpapering her bedroom and then begin on the paintwork.

In a moment she would go and make herself a cup of tea. She would drink it at the pine table in the kitchen and read up on the basics of taming a cottage garden. She could easily grow all her own vegetables here. And with a roof over her head, and food in the garden, she would perhaps only need a part-time job to keep the wolf from the door.

And then she would paint and paint and paint!

She would paint the cottage in all lights and in all seasons. She would paint the wide East Anglian horizons and the ploughed fields and the sun among the clouds!

'Oh!'

Luxuriously she stretched her arms high into the quiet blue above her and threw back her head. Life would begin to be good again. She could feel it.

Then she heard the noise. High up and far away, the smallest buzz of an engine, like an angry wasp.

Shading her eyes she quartered the sky until finally she saw it.

Way away, beyond the hidden village, probably miles away, a tiny speck in the blueness, its stubby wings just visible. Lazily it circled, seeming at one with the calm of the mellow evening. But as she watched it suddenly dived down and steeply up again, turning on to its back and speeding down to form a perfect loop, then another and another, before breaking into breathtaking turns and figures of eight.

It was beautiful to watch. Sometimes it seemed to hang suspended for one heart-stopping moment before pivoting around one wing and plummeting earthwards again.

She watched for a long time, until the sun dipped almost to the horizon. It was frightening and exhilarating at the same time, like an aerial ballet which the little aeroplane was performing for its own delight.

But the note of the engine sounded angry, and she knew without any telling who was in the cockpit, and what private fury he was intent on working out of his system.

CHAPTER TWO

THE next day was a perfect autumn day, and a productive one. By lunchtime the papering in the main bedroom was finished.

She stepped back to admire the effect.

'Not bad for a beginner,' she said to herself, and wiped wallpaper paste from her hands by rubbing them vigorously down her old painting smock. Almost immediately she set to work clearing up and retouching the white gloss paint. There was only the window frame and the door and the skirting board to attend to; with luck it would be finished that day. Three years ago, when she was just twenty-one, she had learned that there was nothing like backbreaking work to block unpleasant thoughts during the day, and to induce exhausted sleep at night.

So now she hardly ever thought consciously about Simon, or their marriage, or the fatal accident which ended it. Only in dreams did it sometimes come back to force her awake, trembling and sobbing.

The door and window were quickly finished. She was kneeling down, tackling the last tricky corner of skirting board, when the voice made her yelp with surprise.

'Mrs Passmore.'

'What in heaven's name are you doing here! In my cottage! In my *bedroom*!' She jumped up and gesticulated angrily with her paint brush. 'And don't call me that, either. My name's Cindy. Everyone calls me Cindy.' Surprise and anger made her blurt out her irritation. He was standing in the doorway, hands pushed down into his jeans' pockets, as if he had every right to be there.

'I didn't mean to startle you. I knocked but no one answered. I heard you working, but I guess you didn't hear me coming upstairs.'

15

'You guessed right,' she said grimly, and pointedly returned to her painting. But she could sense him behind her, watching her every movement, and it made her want to scream with tension.

'Mrs—Cindy—I hate asking for anything. Let alone twice. But when it's a question of safety, then I'll go crawling to anyone. I beg you—please—let me build that runway.'

It was ironic really. His pleading sounded like other people's lazy arrogance. He was a proud man, and everything in his voice made her aware that he knew right was on his side.

'No,' she said through gritted teeth, without raising her head from her painting. 'No. I told you yesterday, it's impossible.'

'Nothing's impossible, if you want it enough,' he said curtly. 'I must have that runway. I *will* have it.'

Something in his voice, like cold steel, made her shudder.

'Here.' To her surprise he was suddenly kneeling beside her, taking the brush from her hand. 'Your hand's shaking so much you're about to ruin your beautiful wallpapering.'

Deftly he slicked an even layer of paint along the wood.

'Oh!' Exasperated, she jumped up and paced the room. 'How dare you just walk into my house like this?'

'My house.' The phrase felt strange on her lips.

He looked sideways up at her, through dark lashes. 'If you don't want people walking in, don't leave the door open in invitation. Someone else has been here as well. There's a dozen eggs in the kitchen, and an invitation to tea from Mrs Evans.'

'Oh.' She looked at him doubtfully. In London she had always been careful to lock her door, but here it hadn't seemed to matter. But she *was* living alone—and word about that seemed to have spread quickly enough.

He grinned a little grimly. 'Don't look so worried. Betty Evans is the village shopkeeper, not some rampaging psychopath. There, that's about it.' He popped the brush into the jar of turps which she had set neatly on a newspaper, and got up. 'Don't leave those brushes in that for too long,' he warned. 'It can make them go soft.'

'I know,' she hissed at him. 'If there's one thing I *do* know about, it's brushes and paint.'

Calmly he wiped his hands—strong, expressive hands, she noticed—on his jeans. Both the faded denims and the check cotton shirt he wore were well fitting enough to show a powerful, athletic frame.

She swallowed, blinked and determinedly looked away. Her hands were still shaking. She wanted him to go away and leave her in peace.

'So the easel in the hall must be yours,' he said.

'Ten out of ten.'

He looked around, his eyes taking in a suitcase full of tumbled underthings, all white lace and cotton, and going slowly over the three-quarter size bed, with its apple green duvet cover.

'This is a pretty room,' he said, 'for one. How about offering me a cup of coffee?'

The sight of his eyes on her bed, the thoughts that had quite obviously strayed casually through his mind—and which he had not bothered to conceal—spread a warmth of embarrassment through her.

'No,' she said. 'Get out.'

How dare he, she thought. How *dare* he! Not that her bad temper had any effect.

'If you offer me a cup of coffee,' he said evenly, 'I'll fix your front door—and your back door. There's too much work here for a girl on her own.'

'I don't need your help with anything, Mr Seaton,' she flashed. 'Anything you do for me will simply be to blackmail me into changing my mind about your runway. Well you needn't bother to try, because it will just be wasted effort!'

'Oh, yes?' He came and stood close before her, a taunting light in his dark eyes. 'Well then why are you so worried? Why not set me to work, get some hard labour for nothing, and then turn me down flat at the end of it?'

Her eyes were held by his challenging gaze.

'Because I'm not like that,' she said coldly. 'Whatever you might think of me, I don't treat people that way. Anyway, I can manage perfectly well on my own. I'm quite capable of it—and I like my privacy.'

The word fell between them like a stone. She could have bitten her tongue off.

'Ah, yes,' he spat out contemptuously. 'The prized privacy! So precious that you can't even find the generosity to let the occasional pilot fly over at eight hundred feet.'

His eyes raked her face until she felt naked and flayed. 'I can't believe that someone who looks so pretty and sweet could be so totally cold and inhuman. I suppose you gave your husband the push, as well, so you could be quite alone in your country hideaway!'

There was a terrible moment of deathly silence. Then a wracked gasp of pain was wrung from her as he turned and went quickly down the steep cottage stairs.

'Oh!'

Blind and stumbling she groped her way to the bed and flung herself across it, struck down by a dreadful tidal wave of pain and hurt. Huge gulps of scalding sobs tore past her throat, making her body shake with despair.

How *could* he have known? How had he been able, in one short contemptuous sentence, to touch the very centre of her guilt and loss?

Hands clutched tight against her wet cheeks she cried and cried until her body was an empty shell. Then she lay for a long, long time exhausted, too limp to think coherently, until her tears dried and she was able to lift her head.

Slowly, stiffly she went to the bathroom and rinsed her face in cold water. Over the past three years she had schooled herself to carry on, even when it seemed impossible. She made her way downstairs.

Jake was sitting at the kitchen table waiting for her.

'Look, I'm sorry,' he said. He got up and took her elbow and she let him lead her to the table and to a chair he pulled out for her. She was too emotionally exhausted to be surprised he was there.

'That was utterly unforgivable of me,' he said. 'My only excuse is that I so desperately need to build that runway. Even so, I had no right to——'

'Please.' She put her swollen face into her hands. 'I don't want to talk about it any more.'

There was a long silence.

'My husband was killed in a car accident,' she said through her fingers. 'It happened three years ago. We were only married a few months.'

There was another endless silence. Then she felt strong, gentle fingers taking her hands from her face. His eyes were on her, serious and concerned, but also closely reading her mood.

'I'm sorry, Cindy. You must have had it so hard.' His hand held hers for a moment. Then he was pushing a cup across the table.

'I made some tea. Drink it, you'll feel better.'

It was true, the hot liquid began to revive her. Colour crept back into her face.

'Now,' said Jake. 'Where's your tool box? I'll fix those doors.'

'Please——' She began to protest, but she knew it was useless. And somehow it was curiously comforting to yield up difficult tasks to someone else—a luxury she had not allowed herself for years.

'I've only got the basics. They're in a green bag on the floor in the living room. But don't you have things to do?'

'I'm the boss. My instructors don't need me breathing down their necks all the time. And you must allow me to do something to try and make amends.'

He went off and she sat and listened to him moving around in the next room. It was a curious feeling to have someone else in the cottage, but not an entirely unpleasant one. At least, it wouldn't be, if the person were anyone but Jake Seaton. But he seemed to have an infinite capacity to upset her, and he had made it quite plain what he thought of her. If he was being nice to her now it was only—as he said—to make amends.

He returned at that moment, car keys in hand.

'No big screwdriver,' he said. 'But I've got one. And I'll get some oil for those hinges. Do you need anything else?'

She shook her head and he was gone in a moment, striding quickly out of the door. Then she heard his car roar into life.

On a sudden impulse she jumped up and ran upstairs. From the bedroom window under the eaves she could just see a white Alfa Romeo disappearing around the bend in the lane.

When he returned she had started work on the back bedroom. He called out to reassure her who it was, but left her undisturbed. Occasionally at first she heard him moving around downstairs, but with the dormer window flung open she heard the chorus of birdsong more than she heard anything within the cottage. Late afternoon sun flooded in with the scents and sounds of the garden and slowly peace returned to her. By the time the light began to fade the worst of the papering was done. She laid down her wallpapering brush and crossed to look out over the dusky garden.

In London there had never been much to look at except other people's drainpipes. Although during those brief months of marriage there had been the spectacular view across the city from the smart high-rise Kensington flat which had been Simon's bachelor home.

Those days usually seemed far away now. But then— as now—she had often crossed to the window at dusk and stood looking out. Only then her thoughts had been always centred on Simon, wondering why he was always so late coming home; why she felt almost lonely when she should have been one of the happiest people on earth.

'Surveying the estate?'

'Oh!' She jumped. 'Why are you always doing that to me?'

'Why are you always so lost in your own thoughts?' he replied lightly.

He was almost directly behind her, looking out over her shoulder, enormously tall in the low-ceilinged room. 'Do you realise what time it is? You've worked for five hours without a break.'

'I thought you would have gone by now.'

He grinned down at her, a crooked, careless grin. 'You mean, you hoped I would have gone by now?'

She shrugged, feigning indifference. But with the evening closing in it was really quite nice to have someone there. Even if he did make her feel both angry and almost fearful, both at the same time.

'You've done all this this afternoon?' The wallpaper roses glimmered in their fresh colours.

She looked around with satisfaction. 'Yes.' It *did* look nice. She hugged her elbows and eyed her labours. 'Tomorrow I'll finish this room. Then I can polish the floors upstairs, put the rugs down and get the furniture straight and everything will be ready for the weekend.'

'Visitors?'

'A friend. Coming to lend a hand.'

'A special friend?' He raised an eyebrow.

She smiled. 'Oh yes. Very special.'

'Well,' he said lightly, turning to look around, 'I hope he realises what hard work you've put in to get things ready.'

There was a pause. Perhaps it would be useful to let him think she had a boyfriend? But this was a small society. Word would get round soon enough. And why should she feel any *need* for deceit?

'It's not a he, it's a she,' she said, gathering together her brushes and paste bucket.

'Ah, I see,' he said in a deadpan voice, and took the bucket from her hand.

They clattered down the bare stairs.

'The carpet's coming next week,' she said, unnecessarily. It was nothing to do with him. At the bottom of the stairs she flicked the light switch and suddenly gasped. All the floorboards in the living room and the hall had been renovated. New nails replaced rusty and missing ones and the half-a-dozen splintered planks had been replaced by new boards. It was a job she had been dreading, but now it was done.

'You——?' She turned to him and almost bumped her nose on his chest.

'It needed doing. And I had some spare wood at the club. The doors are both done as well.'

It was true. The front door swung invitingly open without its habitual squawk of protest, and the back door was the same. All the bolts and latches were oiled and shining, in mint condition.

She turned to Jake. 'You shouldn't have bothered. But I'm very grateful.'

He made a mock half-bow. 'My pleasure, ma'am. Of should I say Cindy?'

When he smiled his eyes grew warmer, and his deep voice saying her name made her heart skip a beat. She walked quickly into the kitchen.

'Our first two meetings haven't exactly been a wild success,' he said. 'Can I propose we start again, and get to know each other properly, as two civilised human beings?'

'What do you mean?'

She ran water briskly into the sink and began to wash out the paste bucket. Civilised hardly seemed the right adjective for him, although it seemed he could be charming when he chose. He leaned easily against the draining board beside her, ankles casually crossed, and his presence was definitely disturbing, making her extra brisk at her work.

The old habit of defensiveness. She would get involved with no one, ever again, she had decided. That way no one caused hurt, and no one got hurt. She was quite capable of managing on her own, and to prove it she scrubbed energetically at the bucket, soaking herself and him in the process.

Without a word he reduced the wild flow of water from the tap. 'What I mean is, what are you doing now? This evening?'

Her heart began to knock with apprehension. She swallowed the dryness from her throat. 'I'm going to have a bath and wash my hair. Then I'm going to have supper, and then I'm going to finish the bedroom curtains.'

She shook the upturned bucket over the sink and looked around for a drying cloth. It was hanging from a peg just to one side of him. Carefully, with her eyes down, she reached gingerly around his hips and unhooked it, then stepped back in haste, busily drying out the bucket.

'I don't bite,' he said, his eyes on her. He added, 'No, you're not.'

She looked at him, startled.

'You've worked like a trooper all day. You haven't had any lunch, and you probably haven't had much breakfast and if you stay here you'll only nibble a boiled egg and some lettuce.' With a flourish he opened her fridge. 'There you are, eggs and lettuce. And not much more in your cupboards, I've checked.'

'Well it was half-day closing in the village today——'

He cut her off. 'I'm not casting aspersions on your housekeeping. Good God, you've hardly had time to draw breath. I just don't want to see you fade away altogether. So I'll pick you up at eight and take you out for a proper meal. All right?'

It was obvious he wasn't going to take no for an answer. Dumbly she nodded. Then his eyes were on her face, reading its expression. 'No,' he added. 'Make that seven. You're tired out and ought to get to bed early.'

Her eyes flew to him. The word seemed to lie heavily between them. He laughed shortly. 'Don't look such a frightened fawn. My intentions are at least *fairly* honourable.'

As he left, the door closed behind him without a creak from its newly oiled hinges.

Later, lying in a hot tub of jasmine bath suds, she thought about that last remark. Of course he was taking her out to dinner to try and persuade her to change her mind about the runway. Just as he had worked all afternoon to try and soften her up. Although he had seemed genuinely contrite about the way he had upset her.

She didn't want to think about that, so she scrubbed a knee reflectively and wondered whether she should have accepted the invitation?

The way it had been profered had left little choice, but she could have bolted the door behind him and refused to answer it when he returned.

The trouble was, as least part of her *wanted* to go. She was languid with tiredness. It would be such bliss to enjoy a meal not prepared by herself, and to get away from the disorder of the cottage.

And it had been such a long time since she had been taken out, properly, by a man. In London she had surrounded herself with a group of casual friends and had been very careful not to get close to anyone in particular. Her marriage, and the nightmare months after the accident, had set her apart from people of her own age group, shadowing her face with a deeper knowledge of the world, and it was always easier not to have to explain it all to new faces.

The long and the short of it was that Jake Seaton was a very attractive man, she told herself.

In the kitchen, just before he left, she had been vibrantly aware of him, his ease with himself, the way he looked at her, the gypsy quality about him that showed he was entirely his own master.

Her mind rejected him, knowing what he wanted from her. But her body reacted differently, with a throb of awareness that years of quiet and celibate living had not entirely quieted

Not that she had the slightest intention of becoming involved with him in any way. But his magnetism was strong, and it would be dishonest not to acknowledge that the thought of being wined and dined by him—whatever his motives—was far from unpleasant.

Wrapped in a thick towel she padded through to the bedroom and dried her hair. Some instinctive caution warned her against a dress that left too much of anything exposed. Even so, it was a relief to leave her jeans on one side and to slip into a favourite silky green dress with a high antique lace collar. At her wrist she fastened a gold bracelet which matched the slim band on her left hand. High-heeled strappy sandals accentuated her slim figure and turning in front of the mirror which stood propped against one wall ready for fixing in place, she was pleased with the result.

Normally she wore no make-up, but tonight she emphasised the fine bones of her face with a little light blusher and brushed sooty mascara over the long lashes which fringed her eyes. In the lamp light their green flecks deepened, and the shiny curls which tumbled about her shoulders were mellow auburn.

Jake, when he arrived, did not bother to hide his astonishment.

'Cindy, you look wonderful! But what happened to the female house renovator? I thought I'd be lucky if you put on a clean painting smock!'

He set her back from him, his hand on her shoulder, while he took in her appearance from top to toe. He wore an impeccably cut dark jacket over a white shirt and dark trousers, and looked handsome and imposing. But even the smart clothes failed to tame the air of slightly tousled wildness she had noticed the first time he had stood on her doorstep. The close scrutiny made her colour rise and he laughed, a throaty confident laugh, and brushed his lips lightly over her forehead.

She blinked. It was so quick she did not know if she had imagined it. And there was no time to think about it because Jake was already helping her into her jacket and hurrying her down the cottage path to the low-slung white car.

Inside, driving up the lane, it was a different world. Jake was a superb driver—she sensed it immediately—and although fast cars normally made her nervous, this one nosed along the twisting roads like a well-trained racing horse held in check. A low Beethoven concerto played on the stereo, and conversation seemed entirely unnecessary.

Once Jake glanced over to her and smiled, but mostly he left her to her thoughts. Which, she thought wryly, was altogether a bad thing. Because her thoughts were acutely aware of him, his hands on the leather-covered driving wheel, gently handling the powerful car, his long legs beside her, the glimpse of bronzed wrist below his shirt cuff. It was terrible. Such thoughts had not come to her so strongly for years. Not since Simon, with all the expertise born of wide experience, had first shown her what the delights of love could be all about.

Tightly she gripped her hands in her lap, forcing her eyes to watch only the headlamp-lit road ahead. This was not the time or place to think such thoughts; and Jake Seaton was quite definitely not the right person to think them about.

CHAPTER THREE

'HERE we are.' The car slid to a halt by a thatched country inn. 'The landlord's one of my pupils—and his wife cooks like a dream.'

She looked with relief at the welcoming building, feeling far too tense and tired to face an expensive restuarant.

Jake was given an enthusiastic welcome. A woman bustled out from the kitchen and he bent to kiss her warmly. Free drinks were offered in the bar, but Jake flashed a quick look at her and suggested they go straight through to the dining room.

'I could see you were in no mood for a party,' he told her as large schooners of sherry were set before them. He lifted his glass. 'Here's to a hard day's toil.' His eyes warmed as he crooked a one-sided smile at her and she felt an answering warmth start up beneath her ribs. She smiled tightly and looked swiftly away.

She *mustn't* feel like that about him.

'How do you feel?' he asked, as if he could read her thoughts.

'Oh.' She swallowed. 'All my bones ache, but it's the right kind of tiredness. The virtuous kind.'

'How long do you think it will take you to get the cottage straight?'

'I hope to finish everything by the spring. So I can start on the garden.'

He grinned. 'You?'

Her chin rose. 'Yes. Why not?'

'Oh, no reason.' His face was straight, but his eyes brimmed with amusement. 'It's just that the ground seems pretty packed down in places.'

'So?'

'Well, I suppose you know that soil needs to be

27

turned by at least the depth of a spade to be any good? And it should be done before winter, so the frost can get at it.'

'Oh.' She frowned. Being a property owner was far more demanding than she had imagined. But she would manage.

'Well then, I'll make a start this year. I don't see——'

'Have you ever tried to dig to the depth of a spade?'

'No, but——'

'——you don't see why you can't do it!' He was still gently laughing at her.

'That's right.' Somehow her mouth was crooking back at him. Perhaps he was right to tease her out of her fierce defensiveness.

'Well, I'm sure if you set your mind to it you'll do it. It'll take you a year or two, and you'll end up with muscles like Mr Universe—but you'll do it.'

She looked at him questioningly. 'Will it really be that hard?'

'I would think so. Your aunt was a pretty sick lady when she died. She must have been too frail for heavy work for many years. And it certainly looks a tangle out there.'

'It does, doesn't it? Although when I was little the garden was always full of lupins and canterbury bells and roses. The roses are still there, but they've all gone wild.'

A waiter discreetly handed them two menus.

'Thank you.' She looked at Jake. 'You know, it's years since I've been taken out for anything more than a quick pizza.'

'That's strange,' he said. 'We country bumpkins imagine you city dwellers are always nipping out for lunch at the Savoy.'

She laughed. 'Hardly. Although I did have tea at the Ritz this summer. A Kuwaiti diplomat's wife wanted me to teach her son to draw. I was summoned to discuss my fees. When I saw what she was willing to pay for a cucumber sandwich I doubled them!'

'And did she pay?'

'Yes, but it was cash down the drain, I'm sorry to say. Young Ahmed hadn't a drop of talent, poor lad, and he didn't like art anyway. He just wanted to play football.' The sherry was making her unusually talkative. She lowered her eyes hastily and read down the lengthy menu. Eventually she lifted troubled eyes to Jake. 'Look, I'm terribly sorry, but I really am out of the habit of eating big meals. Would you mind if I just had a grilled steak and a salad?'

'Of course not. I like people who know what they want. Like Ahmed. Although I can recommend the avocado mousse as a light starter, if you can find an odd corner for it.'

The waiter lit their candle and removed the menus.

'It's all very well knowing what you want,' she said, 'as long as you've some hope of getting it. Ahmed hadn't a chance of any football training because his mother had decided he was going to be a great artist. She never let him out to play.'

'How about you? Have you any hope of getting what you want?'

Her eyes met his. 'All I really want is the opportunity to do some serious painting. Having the cottage will make all the difference. Aunt Beth knew that, bless her. I'll have more time now.'

'No more Ahmeds?'

'That's right. It can be fun to teach people with real talent, but mainly it's just a bit of a slog. You must find that, teaching people to fly?'

'I don't do much of that any more. I mostly instruct people who already have quite a bit of experience. And they tend to be quite keen—and quite good. When things go well I get quite a kick out of it, but when they go badly I want to shake the student by the neck and throw him out of the cockpit. I'm not a patient man— as you've probably gathered!'

She pulled a wry face. 'On brief acquaintance, I wouldn't say patience was one of your virtues.'

'In fact you wouldn't have said I had any virtues.' It was a statement, not a question.

'No. I would have said you were very good at laying floorboards and mending doors.'

His eyes glinted with wicked humour. 'Ah, but that's only the beginning. There are no end to my talents once I get started.'

Her heart started to knock dangerously, and instinctively her lips tightened into a frosty smile. 'I dare say, but I'll take your word for it.'

'Oh,' he said in a low voice, his eyes holding hers, 'that's a pity.'

Luckily their meal arrived before the tell-tale flush could creep unhindered to her cheeks, and as they ate their mousse she moved swiftly on to other topics.

'How do you know so much about gardening?'

'I once worked for a nursery garden. It was a long time ago, but it taught me the difference between a peony and a pansy.'

'You mean you haven't always been a pilot?'

'No, but pilots sometimes lose their jobs.'

Her eyes widened in surprise. 'Why?'

'Well, this one lost his because he told the man he was working for that his aeroplanes were so poorly maintained they were flying death traps. He ran a crop-spraying firm and he shouldn't have been taking any chances. Low and slow flying—the kind you do when you're spraying—is the most dangerous kind there is. But this was out in South America where no one cares too much about rules and regulations. I was shown the door. Luckily.'

'Why luckily?'

'Because the aeroplane I had been flying, Bravo India, caught fire in mid-air a week later. The man who was flying it was killed in the crash.'

'Oh.' She took a sharp breath. He sounded so matter-of-fact, almost callous.

'In my world things like that sometimes happen. But they shouldn't ever happen because someone's saving pennies on servicing, or cutting back on training. That's when I came to England, and backed out of flying for a time to rethink my position. I pushed barrows of turf around this nursery near here and mulled things over at leisure. In the end I decided it was time I stopped being a rolling stone and became my own boss.'

'That's when you started the club?'

'Yes. There was an airfield close by that wasn't in use, and I thought it might be a good thing to make sure people were properly taught. And it would leave time for my hobby.'

'Which is what?'

He smiled at her, a slow wicked smile.

'Flying.'

'Don't you ever want a change?'

His gaze was suddenly serious. He looked at her for a long moment. 'Flying is a passion,' he said. 'It doesn't leave a man.'

She lowered her eyes, reaching for her wine glass. For some reason her hand was unsteady.

'And like all passions,' he went on, his voice lighter, 'it's expensive, time-consuming—and can play havoc with your peace of mind.'

The meal passed in a haze of food and wine and surprisingly easy conversation. It was a long time since she had found herself relaxing so completely in a stranger's company. Jake told her how he had grown up in New Zealand and trained as an airline pilot just as soon as he was old enough. After five years he had had enough of the starchy gold-braided world of international airlines and had taken off for a succession of places and jobs.

Her first impression had been right. He had been footloose and fancy free, making the most of life, going where the fancy took him. He had flown mails in Africa, and company executives around the Middle East. He made her laugh with stories of characters he had worked with, and things he had seen, and she was gripped by his description of the emergency flying doctor flights he had helped with.

With the coffee he ordered two cognacs.

'Don't drink it if you don't want to, but it will help you get a good night's sleep.'

She sipped it cautiously. The wine was already making her head spin, and the amber liquid spread a mellow glow inside her. Life looked very good, she thought hazily. The future looked rosy.

Jake lit a cheroot and leaned back in his chair.

'And you?' he said, turning the conversational tide. 'What about you?'

Her eyes grew wary, their green flecks darkening. 'There's nothing to tell.' The words came out quickly. 'You know what I do.'

'I know what you do. Not who you *are*.' His voice was low and mellow, like the brandy, melting her defences.

She twisted the stem of her glass. 'I'm Cindy Passmore. I'm twenty-four. I'm an artist—at least, I hope to be one day——'

'Did you train to be one?'

'I went to art school for three years, but in the end I didn't take the final exams.' Even after all these years a note of bitterness crept into her voice. 'My mother always disapproved of artists. When I left for college in London she more or less washed her hands of me. I only saw her a few more times before she died, a year later. I could understand how she felt. She'd had a hard life, bringing me up on my own because my father hadn't been around since I was born. She hoped I would do something secure and well-paid . . . After that I stayed in the city all the time. I worked in the holidays to earn money for the next term. The grant I got barely covered my tube fares.'

'It sounds a struggle.'

'It was, in a way.' Struggle was the word, she thought. It wasn't difficult to remember what it had been like to get up before dawn to get over to the smart Mayfair hotel to carry up early morning teas. Then there was the Saturday store work in Oxford Street, with her ankles swelling over her shoes by the end of each long, tiring day. And the hospital where she had washed dishes and made friends with a Ugandan engineering student who had taught her Swahili and kept her going with his jokes. Thinking of him, she said: 'But it was worth it. And it taught me a lot about life. I made some good friends and learned how to fend for myself.'

'And after all that, you didn't finish your course?'

'No. I married instead. Simon lectured in design at my college. He said it would be embarrassing for him to have his wife there, as a student.'

She frowned, remembering their first real argument when she had burst out: 'But you *can't* be serious! I've only got one term left before I take my exams! You *can't* want me to give it all up!' But he had, and so she did.

'Why?' Jake asked bluntly. 'Why would it have been so difficult?' His eyes were hard, his jaw set. With a shiver she remembered his anger of the previous day.

'It's—it's difficult to explain. Simon was a very proud man. He liked everything to be just so. He wanted his life to be—ordered, I suppose, and that meant having his home life quite separate from his working day.'

Sometimes it had seemed that Simon resented the way she had upset that order. It hadn't been in his plans to get married. He had enjoyed being a smart young bachelor about town, with his name appearing regularly in the gossip columns.

His own furniture design company was successful and lecturing was only a small part of his professional life, but it was one he greatly enjoyed. He was blond and willowy and sensual, and all the girl students had fallen instantly in love with him.

Only Cindy had been unmoved, so absorbed was she in her studies. It was her initial coolness that had aroused his interest, then his pursuit. When she finally let him take her out he courted her with a heady mixture of contempt and ardour. His knowledge of his

subject satisfied a burning hunger inside her to know
more of her field of study, but he sometimes brushed
away her earnest questions with lofty impatience,
making her feel young and foolish.

He had wanted to take her to bed. She had refused.
Eventually he had said, 'Well, my girl, if you insist on
being so old fashioned, I suppose there is only one thing
for it.'

They had married quietly the next week.

She had been stunned when he told her she could not
finish her studies, but he had held her tightly and said,
'Don't I mean more to you, Cindy?' and had made love
to her until her thoughts whirled and there was no time
to make the obvious reply, 'Do they have to be
exclusive?'

Later he had refused to discuss the subject and the
days in his penthouse flat had crawled slowly past until
she felt as trapped as a young animal that has
thoughtlessly given up its freedom for a few pats on the
head.

Now she rested her brandy glass against her chin and
looked across at Jake, as dark as Simon had been fair,
and broad and strong as Simon had been slender. It was
astonishing how easy this stranger was to talk to, she
thought hazily.

'On the last day of the exams I walked past the
college,' she told him dreamily. 'It was a beautiful
summer's day and everyone was just coming down the
steps, laughing and talking. I stood on the other side of
the road and watched them, all my friends, discussing
how they had done, and I vowed to myself then that,
whatever happened, I would still become an artist. Not
necessarily a good one, but the best one I could possibly
be.'

Her eyes focused on the present again, on Jake
looking at her with dark attention, and she smiled self-
consciously. 'Does that sound silly?'

'No. You must show me your paintings.'

'They're not very good. I'm still learning.'

'If you're really serious about something, you never stop learning till the day you die.'

'Like you and flying?'

He grinned. 'I learn something every day.'

She excused herself as he paid the waiter. In the cloakroom mirror her eyes sparkled with life and liveliness.

'You're drunk!' she whispered to her becomingly flushed reflection and giggled a little. Everything was slightly dreamy, but why not? How long was it since she had been taken out to dinner by a handsome man who listened sympathetically and had just the right degree of curiosity and tact? She pulled a face. Sympathy? Tact? Jake Seaton? She giggled again. Who on earth would have thought she would have used those words about him when he had appeared in her bedroom doorway earlier today?

Carefully she repaired her lipstick. Jake had firm even lips that crooked engagingly to one side when he smiled. His teeth were white against his dark eyes and hair. When he laughed he looked wicked and carefree, like a pirate or a gypsy, but his profile, with its straight nose and firm chin, was serious and stubborn. He was a man with a strong will, and a strong body. He could be dangerous, she was sure, and he was certainly determined. He was determined to make her change her mind about the runway, and that was why he had taken her out to dinner and been so thoroughly charming to her. The rapport between them had been carefully engineered for his own ends.

She *had* to think about that, and not about how his gentle teasing made her feel warm inside, nor about the look in his eyes as they rested on her bare shoulders or hair. Out in the fresh air she shivered a little and Jake took her elbow. It felt wonderful, firm and reassuring, although she tried not to relax too closely against him as they walked to the car.

She was helped into the deep leather seat and once they were driving along found herself watching mesmerised as the hedgerows slipped past in the light of the headlamps. Every bone in her body ached with pleasant exhaustion. She felt languid and at peace with the world.

'Cindy?'

'Mmm.'

'Don't be alarmed. I'm going to take a bit of a detour. There's something I must check on at the club.'

Automatically her drooping eyelids flew open wide. Alarm signals rang in her head. So he was just like all the others, all the men she had so determinedly kept at bay since her marriage ended! But Jake just laughed at her expression.

'I told you not to be alarmed. I'm not going to "run out of petrol" then ravish you in a layby. I'm far too old for that sort of game.' He changed gear smoothly as the car began to nose down a narrow lane. 'Anyway,' he added conversationally, 'I've never yet found it necessary. Thank goodness for women's liberation, or some of it at least. Nowadays people can be far more honest about what they want from each other, without it all hooked to the inevitable marriage contract. I bet a few thousand lives have been made happier by that.'

She flashed him a covert glance, but his profile was expressionless. It seemed he had told the truth when he said he was not out to seduce her. Peversely she felt a stab of disappointment. But as her eyes began to close again she wondered sleepily about his words.

Simon had conjured up depths of desire in her she had not known existed, but it had never occurred to her to say anything but no to his entreaties. Was that why they had married? Perhaps if things had been different their relationship would have been only a brief affair, not a bitter marriage . . . And then they might not have had that terrible final row . . . And Simon would not have slammed angrily out into the night . . . And his car would not have swerved across the motorway . . .

She was sliding down into the blackness of that night, imagining for the millionth time the headlights as they must have come speeding towards him. Simon, drunk and upset, crashing head-on with an articulated lorry . . .

'No! No!'

'Cindy! What is it?'

She sat up, a hand to her head. Jake's hand was on her shoulder, steadying her.

'You screamed.'

'Did I? I'm sorry . . .' She shook her head and it cleared. She was in a car with Jake Seaton. The accident was years ago. Simon was dead, and it was all her fault.

Jake slowed the car and pulled up. He took her hand. 'You're trembling. Are you all right?'

'Yes, really, thank you.' She took her hand away, praying he would not press her for an explanation. 'I was half-asleep. It must have been a nightmare. I'm fine now, honestly.'

He gave her a long, concerned look, but only said, 'We're at the airfield. I'll get you a rug to wrap around you. What I've got to do won't take a minute.'

His door slammed. It was quiet and calm, but dark. She began to wish he would hurry back. It was ridiculous. She hardly knew him, yet she missed him. His presence was reassuring. It kept the bad dreams at bay.

Against the skyline was a low building with one square of yellow light. That was where Jake was, she thought, and jumped with surprise when he was suddenly beside her.

'Here.' He tucked a soft woollen blanket around her with care, as if she were a sick child, and the action touched her so that she had to blink back tears which sprang to her eyes.

'Thank you. Did you leave a light on?'

'No.' He sounded grim. 'Alan Jenkins, one of my young instructors, is camping out there until he finds somewhere to live. He's just moved down here from up north. Silly young twerp completely forgot about locking up the hangars. It's a good job I checked or anyone could have got in.'

His angry profile made her very glad she wasn't Alan Jenkins. Jake was no man to get on the wrong side of ... although she already had! For a moment the business of the runway had quite slipped her mind.

'Poor Alan Jenkins. Did you give him a hard time?'

'No more than he deserved. Anyway, it's water off a duck's back with him. He could be a first-class pilot, but I'm afraid he's a bit too cocky for his own good.'

'Anyone can make a mistake,' she put in gently.

'I know,' he said, 'but the important thing is whether you learn from them. And he doesn't even seem to try.'

CHAPTER FOUR

THE car slid to a stop at her front gate.

'It doesn't look very welcoming,' Jake observed. 'Are you sure you don't mind living alone?'

He was right. The cottage looked dark and deserted. She swallowed.

'No, I like it. I really do.'

He grinned. She saw the white gleam of his teeth in the darkness.

'Who are you trying to convince?'

He walked up the path with her and took the key to unlock the door. 'Ah, such workmanship,' he exclaimed, as the door opened smoothly.

'I haven't thanked you properly for everything you did this afternoon—and for a lovely evening.'

Jake was a dark shape next to her as she stood in the cottage doorway.

'Then thank me now,' he said softly, and with an easy movement he stepped to her and took her in his arms.

His kiss, on her lips, was light and brief. He had released her before she had even realised what was happening. But the embrace released such a flood of yearning sweetness in her that she stood dazed and trembling, wordless, as he set off down the path. Halfway to the gate he paused. 'Put the light on Cindy, I don't like leaving you in the dark.'

'What?'

'Put the light on.'

'Oh. Yes.'

Still dazed she turned and felt for the hall switch. When she pressed it down nothing happened.

'What's the matter?'

'I think the bulb must have gone.'

He came back, checked the switch, then reached up and unscrewed the bulb. It tinkled as he shook it.

'It's gone all right. Have you got a spare?'

'Yes, I'll get it.'

She felt her way to the living room and stepped cautiously into the room, feeling for the light switch. It wasn't where she remembered it, and she edged further in.

'Ow!'

There was a packing case where there shouldn't be one and she had half-stumbled on it, catching her elbow on the sharp metal corner.

'What is it?'

'Nothing,' she gasped, but Jake was beside her.

'Let me see.'

'No, there's nothing to see.' She hugged her elbow to her chest. 'I banged my arm, but it's nothing.'

'How do you know,' he pointed out logically, 'when you've still got your jacket on?' He reached out and clicked the light switch. The room remained in darkness. 'Do *none* of the lights in the place work?'

'Oh, I forgot! I couldn't find the spare bulbs the other evening, so I used the bulb from here for my bedside light.'

Now that her eyes had grown used to the dim moonlight, she could see quite a lot. She could see that in Jake's look there was exasperation and amusement in about equal measures.

'Take your jacket off and let me see at least if you've drawn blood.'

As if to make sure his instructions were obeyed he stepped closer and eased the coat from her shoulders. Laying it on the packing case, he took her arm, one hand holding her outstretched wrist, the other probing gently along the soft flesh of her inner arm and around her elbow. His touch sent exquisite tremors of pleasure shuddering through her, obliterating all pain. She could hardly breathe.

Jake said softly: 'There's nothing wrong there.' But his hand still cupped her elbow and he looked at her in the thin silver light. Then his hand moved on up the silky skin of her arm, and his other hand pulled her to him.

She did not resist, she did not want to.

Slowly and deliberately he took her in his arms and found her lips. It was different, this time, from that other casual farewell on the doorstep, but the sweet forgotten warmth that started up inside her was the same. Hesitantly her lips parted beneath his. Her hands went up to his shoulders. Under her hands she felt the well-cut lie of his suit, and under that the firm muscles of a man in the peak of condition.

His embrace was everything her straying thoughts had imagined, and more. She could not have known how much her lips would love the feel of his firm, even lips against them, nor how much her body would want to move closer to his.

As if knowing this, Jake pulled her closer still. His hands went up to tangle in her hair and his kiss was harder, more demanding.

She should stop him now, she knew she should. But it was impossible. No man had touched her for three years, but she was young and healthy and normal, and Jake Seaton had simply walked straight through her defences.

Her hands moved with a will of their own, under his jacket to feel the planes of his shoulders through the thin material of his shirt. He kissed her eyes and ears and laid trails of longing down to the hollow of her neck, until she gasped at the exquisite molten pleasure he could rouse in her.

When his lips found hers again it was with a savage sweetness that seemed to go through to the very heart of her being. She was lost to him. Her lips opened to his, as his tongue took its freedom, finding her and knowing her. His hands moulded her against him, leaving her in no doubt about how greatly he desired her, and the knowledge was like a drug that made her head spin and her hands move to draw him closer.

'Oh!' Jake groaned and tore his lips from hers. 'Cindy.'

His dark eyes searched her face, her eyes huge and luminous, her lips crushed from his passion. She could have pulled away from him then. Dimly her whirling thoughts told her that was so. But the blood was drumming in her veins and she wanted to stay forever in his arms. Her face tilted up to him and he was kissing her again, deeply, holding her close, while her hands went up to his thick dark hair, to pull him down to her. One of his hands moved to stroke her neck, her shoulder, and down over the fullness of her breast. She shuddered and arched herself towards him, her body tightening under his touch. Then he was slipping open the buttons of her dress, finding the warm flesh beneath her lacy bra, feeling her breast swell and harden beneath his hand as he kissed the secret hollows beneath her hair and held her against the whole hard length of him.

She could feel his heart beating beneath his shirt, and then somehow his shirt was open and her hands were on his skin, knowing the hair that sprinkled his broad chest, the firm muscles of his shoulders.

'Oh——' Unknowing, she cried out softly, with the ache of longing he aroused in her. When she buried her head against him, she smelt the distinctive maleness of him, so alien from her feminine world, and her heart hammered so loudly she was sure he must feel it as his two hands caressed both her breasts.

'We must get rid of these clothes,' he groaned softly against her ear, and with an arm about her he led her surely to where he knew her bedroom to be.

An icy finger of panic reached out towards her as they went together up the dark cottage stairs. This shouldn't be happening, it said! It was all wrong!

But when Jake took her in his arms again, it seemed that nothing he could do could be wrong. He kissed her tenderly, almost as if he sensed her fears, and hers were the arms that tightened first, with the urgent need to meld and fuse. Yet his passion was strained to the limit, and quickly flared.

Locked together, the world forgotten, he slid the dress down from her shoulders and unhooked her bra. He bent to kiss the curves of her breasts, the sensitive tips, rousing her to the brink of desire. Impatiently she reached to help him rid himself of jacket and shirt. When they kissed again her warm flesh met his with a shock of delight. It shouldn't happen. It was not how she behaved. But it was going to. And it was too late to worry or care. And, anyway, she wanted it to happen. She wanted Jake, she wanted to give herself to his man's needs ... She wanted him to help her from her dress, and for his hands to know all her body's sweetness ... And for him to ease her into bed ... and then to swiftly join her, his lean muscled nakedness against her, as he gathered her to him tenderly, whispering her name. After that there were no more words. Jake held her safe as he kissed and caressed her, his hands learning the curves of her breasts and hips, his lips exploring her skin. And it all felt so right, so utterly right, as she moved closer to him, knowing how much he wanted her, and how he held himself back for her.

And if what was happening now, between them, was not what the world would think quite proper, then it didn't matter. Because she was melting with exquisite tenderness, and the blood was singing in her veins, and her defences were finally gone so that she yearned to give herself completely in an affirmation of life. And what was happening, the touching and finding and longing, was between the two of them, private and precious, shielded by the privacy of her own, her very own house ...

Her eyes flew open. Every muscle in her body stiffened in instinctive defence.

How could she be such a fool!

'No! No!'

It was the worst possible moment, almost too late.

Jake drew away as if she had rained blows about his head. He said nothing.

It was one of the most terrible moments of her life. She had betrayed Aunt Beth, betrayed Rose Cottage. Jake Seaton wanted permission to build his runway, and he would stop at nothing to get it. And just seconds ago she had been about to let him make love to her. If that had happened he would have undoubtedly used it against her. She would have been in his power. He could have ruined her reputation locally. He would most certainly have got his own way. No doubt that was why he had taken her out tonight. And when he saw what a gift of an opportunity she was prepared to lay before him, he had seized it with all too obvious pleasure.

Jake propped himself on one elbow and looked at her. 'What is it?' His voice was non-commital.

'You—you——' She was incoherent with rage at herself and him. Every limb trembled with loss and embarrassment. Flashing a look at him she saw his eyes go over her exposed breasts and, blushing deeply, she pulled the duvet up round her.

'Yes?' His voice told her he expected her to account for herself.

Her thoughts were churning too fast for her to organise a proper sentence. She had not quite been fool enough to let herself think he could care for her. But when he first kissed her, such a tide of electricity had flowed between them that it had been impossible not to believe there was something extraordinary between them. And after that, there had been no thought at all ... she had followed all too willingly where he led, too foolish to realise exactly why he was leading her that way.

'You—I know what you wanted.'

'I would have thought that was perfectly obvious. At least to anyone who know the simplest facts of life.' His voice was hard, angry.

If only she could get out of this terrible, compromising situation. But, lying in bed with this stranger, her brain simply refused to operate.

'No, not that—I mean you're just using me, you just want to take advantage.'

With a very blunt epithet, Jake flung back the covers and got up. She did not look, but heard him climbing into his clothes. She shut her eyes and prayed he would be gone, but he had no intention of letting her off lightly.

When he turned to stand by the bed, she could sense that his fury was barely contained. 'I don't think "taking advantage" would be the interpretation most people would put on what has just happened,' he ground out. He paused, and she was forced to meet his hard, furious stare.

With his jacket over his shoulder, his shirt open at the neck and his gypsy hair tousled, he looked rugged, ruthless—and impossibly handsome.

As ever, he seemed to read her thoughts.

'You gave me every reason to suppose that you wanted to, shall I say *explore* our relationship every bit as much as I did. So don't try and blame me if you get a last-minute attack of doubt. Luckily for you I am at least something of a gentleman. Because if I wasn't, I'd come right back to bed—and I can guarantee that within minutes I'd have you crying out something quite different from the words I just heard.'

'That's a disgusting thing to say!'

'Maybe it is—but maybe so is subjecting other people to every inconsistent whim of behaviour that crosses your mind.'

'Get out!'

'Don't worry,' he said grimly. 'I can hardly wait. But I just want to say one thing. And that is that you are quite the most selfish person I've met in a long time, Cindy Passmore. You're selfish enough to put your personal comfort before other people's safety, and selfish enough to think only of yourself in more—personal matters.'

'You know nothing about my feelings.'

'No, maybe I don't. And now I think I don't want to. Over dinner you seemed, well, quite different, but back on your home territory it's the same old story.'

'Get out. I don't ever want to see you again.'

'That won't be difficult to arrange. But before I go——' He moved swiftly round the bed, tipped her chin up roughly and took her lips brutally with his own. It seared through her, starting up her pulses instantly. But it was over in a second. 'Something to remember me by.' His voice was harsh with bitterness. 'A goodbye kiss.'

Behind him the door shut firmly.

CHAPTER FIVE

SHE woke early and unrested. The events of the night before seemed like a terrible nightmare. But they were all too horribly real.

'Oh no!'

She buried her head in shame under the pillow, but it did not help. She could still remember every last detail of what had happened.

She could remember how eagerly she had responded to his embrace. How she had arched herself to him as his hand found her breast. Together they had lain naked in this bed, this very bed, and known each other length to length. Her hands remembered the lithe beauty of his limbs. With a hot flush of embarrassment, she remembered touching him, making him groan with delight. And how she had wanted to cry out when his skilled caresses had roused her beyond thought.

It had seemed so good, so special. But it wasn't.

It was just that after three years of celibacy her body had flared into passion. And she had heedlessly allowed the first man who kissed her to sweep her off to bed.

No. It was worse than that. She had allowed Jake Seaton to sweep her off to bed, even though she knew he wanted something from her—and had vowed to get it.

No wonder there had been such contempt in his voice when he left. It was no more than she deserved. Her Aunt Beth had left her Rose Cottage, had given her the chance to rebuild her shattered life in peace and tranquillity—and almost immediately she had put all that in jeopardy.

She was wanton and shameless and—yes—selfish. And no matter how deeply she burrowed in the bedclothes, she could not shut out her thoughts.

The phone rang, shattering in the quiet cottage. She looked at her watch. Ten past seven. It was Jake. She could not have said why she was so sure—or what he would want to say to her. Perhaps he intended simply to harangue her into submission over the runway? But she steeled herself not to run down and answer it.

It rang again at eight-thirty, when she was sitting brooding over her morning coffee, and again at ten, and an hour later. By lunchtime her nerves were in tatters. Every time she had to fight not to pick up the receiver.

She hated Jake Seaton, and what he wanted from her, but perversely the longing to hear his voice grew stronger and stronger. She threw herself into finishing the paintwork in the spare bedroom, but instead of seeing the fresh white gloss before her, she saw dark, angry eyes and a contemptuous, arrogant figure.

By afternoon she knew she would have to get out of the cottage or go mad. It was ironic, really. Rose Cottage, which was supposed to be her haven of peace, had turned into a nightmare prison where she was trapped with her own disturbing thoughts.

Yet there was some consolation to be had in the long walk up the lane to the village. The clouds scudded softly along, and the colours of the berried hedgerows made her long for her paintbox. The breeze from the distant sea had a tang of fresh saltiness to it which made her remember she was part of a wider world than her own thoughts and feelings.

After all, everyone made some mistakes in their lives. She had done nothing so very terrible—at least, nothing nearly as terrible as her earlier error in causing Simon to slam out in anger that fateful night. And she had somehow found enough reserves to soldier on through that dark time. She would do the same again. She would work hard, throw herself into her painting, and put Jake Seaton right out of her mind.

The village was sleepily deserted, and the shop bell jangled loudly as she pushed open the door. From the back a youngish woman came hurrying forward.

'Excuse me, I'm looking for Mrs Evans.'

'That's me.'

'Oh goodness! I was expecting someone older. I'm Cindy Passmore, from Rose Cottage. I came to say thank you for the eggs.'

'Betty Evans. I suppose it's the word shopkeeper. It does conjure up visions of steel-rimmed spectacles and sensible brogues, but I'm only thirty-two!' The young woman smiled and extended a welcoming hand and Cindy's spirits lifted as she shook it.

'The eggs were delicious—and it was so nice to have a welcoming note.'

'Well, I know what it feels like to be a newcomer, and country people can be reserved to strangers. I'm from London myself, so I'm probably more used to rubbing shoulders with all types—more of a busybody, my husband Geoff says.'

Betty smiled affectionately at his name. She had a broad, pleasant face and was comfortably dressed in navy trousers and a cream sweater. Cindy felt quite relaxed with her, and found she did not in the least mind the woman's frank appraisal of her jeans and quilted jacket. 'It was your aunt that died, wasn't it? Of course, we didn't know her at all. I think she was just about bedridden when we moved in here, but everyone in the village spoke well of her.'

'She was a lovely lady,' Cindy said warmly. 'She wasn't at all herself towards the end I was told, but I remember her from when I was little and used to stay with her.'

'Yes—I heard something about that. They said she wouldn't let anyone near the house after she got ill, she thought they were going to drag her off to hospital. Apparently she even developed a phobia about aeroplanes, and how people were spying on her from overhead! Still, she had a good innings by all accounts. And it's certainly nice to have a young face in the village. They say too many of the young people round here have to go away and look for work. Mind you,

Geoff and I couldn't wait to leave London.' Betty wrinkled her nose. 'All that noise and dirt. My washing used to get black on the line. Would you like a cup of tea?'

'I'd love one.'

Betty led the way into a cosy living room which looked out on to an immaculately tended garden.

'The shop came with the cottage,' Betty explained over tea and a mouth-watering walnut cake. 'Geoff and I saw it when we drove up from London to look for a house. The shop was all closed up, it had been for a year, and the estate agent kept telling us how we could convert it into a playroom or something. But it seemed such a shame for there to be no shop in the village—especially for all the old people without cars—that I said to Geoff that very night that if he bought the cottage I'd try to get it going again.'

'Did you know anything about shopkeeping?'

'Good Lord, no. But once I'd got the children settled at school, I made some enquiries and found they offered a small-business course at the local college. I went on that for a week, and learned some of the basics. You know, how to keep the books, and set about ordering. After that I learned by trial and error.'

'It looks as if it's thriving—I love the way you have those flowers in buckets outside. It makes you want to stop and call in.'

'Old Mr Hawes grows them on his allotment, bless him. It's his hobby, now he's retired, and we both make a few pennies out of them.' Betty added practically. 'But I've learned I can't keep my prices as low as I'd like. The overheads are just too high. Geoff said he'd underwrite me for the first three months, but after that I'd have to make a profit—or close.'

'What brought you here in the first place?'

Betty laughed. 'My husband—what takes a woman anywhere? He got the chance to work at Haldrome, and he just jumped at it.'

'Haldrome?'

'The airfield, just outside the village. You must have

seen it, it's right near your cottage.'

Cindy's heart began to knock dangerously. Betty poured them both another cup of tea and began to explain.

'Geoff's a maintenance engineer. He looks after aircraft. He worked for years at an aerodrome near north London, servicing air taxi fleets, and it was a good job with good money. But then this job came up at Haldrome and there was no holding him. Luckily, with our two youngsters growing up and wanting to run about and play, we were both ready enough to leave London. And then when we came up for a weekend to sort things out, we both fell in love with the village, and that was it. Within two months we'd packed up and left.'

'But why would he want to work at Haldrome? Isn't it only a little airfield?'

Betty raised a finger. 'Little, but good. Geoff says it's the best flying school in the country. A really smart outfit. People come from all over to learn to fly here. We get top businessmen and actors and all sorts putting up at The Bull and taking lessons. You know Myra Collingdale, the film star? Well she's here often enough.' She grinned broadly. 'Mind you, I think it might be something to do with the extra special tuition she gets. Jake Seaton is quite something.'

'Jake——'

'——Seaton. He runs the airfield and owns the club.'

She swallowed. 'Yes, I've met him.'

'Oh ho,' Betty said roguishly, 'well you know what I mean then. He's quite a head turner—and he's turned Myra Collingdale's head, no mistake about it. Geoff says she's even managed to persuade him to take her up in the Pitts—and that's something he won't do for everyone.'

'The Pitts?'

'Pitts Special. Jake's aerobatic aircraft. It's what Geoff works on, mainly. It's what really brought him up here.'

Cindy looked puzzled. Betty explained, 'Jake Seaton's the absolute tops. He's been the British aerobatic champion for years. I think he's even been world champion. Anyway, he travels everywhere on displays and competitions, and when his last engineer retired he asked Geoff if he'd take over. He knew Geoff was the best in the business,' Betty's voice held real pride, 'and Geoff knew Jake was the best. They make a great team, and Geoff loves the work.'

'Oh, I see. Doesn't it take him away often?' Cindy was unsure whether she was asking about Jake or Geoff. Ever since Betty had mentioned Myra Collingdale an ache of pain had started under her ribs.

'Well, it does rather. But I like to see him so happy. And it keeps me stocked up in duty free perfume! Anyway, being in a village like this is a different thing from being in town. Geoff knows that if anything happened—if I needed help at any time—then everyone would rally round. Having the shop has been great for making friends.'

The telephone rang, and when Betty hurried back there was a worried frown on her face. 'There's trouble at the airfield. That was Geoff. One of the aeroplanes has got an oil leak and Jake wants it fixed tonight. Geoff says he's in an absolutely filthy mood for some reason and everyone's keeping their heads down. Geoff's going to be there till well past seven. It's a nuisance because he promised to fetch the kids from a party they're at in the next village. Now I'll have to find someone else to get them.'

Cindy hesitated. She didn't want to push herself forward, but Betty had been so kind and welcoming. 'If I can be of any help—I mean, I don't drive, but I'd be quite happy to mind the shop while you pop out. That's if you trust me——'

'Trust you. Of course I do!' Betty jumped up and squeezed her shoulder. 'It would be an enormous help, if you really don't mind. Everything's priced, and the till's straightforward.'

'It's all right. I worked in a shop when I was at art school.'

'Art school, gracious.' Beth was shrugging on her jacket, talking breathlessly. 'You know, I've been jabbering on about myself, and you haven't been able to get a word in edgeways. I'm sorry, I'm a bit like that. But you must come round again soon, Cindy, and tell me something about yourself.' She paused in the act of selecting a car key from her key ring and grinned wickedly. 'You do realise, don't you, that you're the talk of the village? After all, it's not every day a beautiful and mysterious young woman moves into one of our romantic thatched cottages. We're all waiting for the handsome stranger to appear on the scene!'

Cindy smiled tightly. He's already here, she thought. And he's already whisked me off my feet. What would Betty think if she had any inkling about last night? But all she said was, 'I'm afraid I'm not at all mysterious, or beautiful. But if you see any handsome strangers around, I wouldn't mind hearing about them.'

Later, as she strolled back down the lane, she mulled over the afternoon's turn of events. She knew instinctively she had found a true and faithful friend in Betty, and it gave her a comfortable feeling to know there was now someone she could turn to for help and advice, a door she could knock on when she was sick of her own company.

There had been no more talk of Jake Seaton, for which she was immensely grateful. She wanted to be alone with herself before she could begin to sort out her confused feelings. There was no doubt about it, the mention of Myra Collingdale had made her sickeningly jealous. But it also meant that Jake had simply been pursuing his own devious aims last night. With a beautiful girlfriend like that, there was no way he could have had even a passing interest in someone like Cindy ... a movement in the lane suddenly caught her eye. A figure was hanging over her front gate, watching her slow progress down the lane. Immediately her thoughts flew to Jake, but there was no car parked in the road, and the figure was too slight, and too friendly looking.

The figure waved energetically.

'This is a fine welcome. I've been sitting on your doorstep for half an hour.'

'Sarah!' Her hand flew in horror to her mouth. 'Oh my goodness! Is it Friday? What's the time?'

Sarah hugged her warmly. 'If you don't mind me saying so, dear Cindy, you seem to be going to pieces somewhat . . .'

'No, I'm not. Don't be ridiculous,' she protested energetically. 'It's just that a lot seems to have happened lately . . .'

'Happened? What on earth happens out here in the sticks? I thought you'd left for a quiet life.'

'I did only——' she hesitated and Sarah looked at her with unconcealed curiosity, '—I've been working so hard on the cottage, and then this afternoon I got roped into helping in the village shop.'

'And that made you forget about your weekend visitor?' Sarah said with obvious scepticism. She picked up her bag and followed Cindy up the path. 'It's funny. I thought it might have something to do with the man who called round just now, looking for you. Tall. Dark. Stunning, in fact. With a nice line in low-slung white sportscars——'

'What?' Cindy paused with the key half in the freshly oiled lock. 'Jake was here?'

'Someone was here. He asked where you were. I said I would like to know, too, since I was supposed to be staying the weekend and didn't much fancy sleeping under the apple trees—he almost grinned at that. I think he might have a sense of humour buried in all that dark fury——'

'Fury?' Cindy asked doubtfully.

'Well, put it like this, I didn't quite catch what he said when he realised you weren't in, but it didn't sound like a terribly long word, or a terribly polite one . . . Then when I announced I was here to stay for a bit he glowered like a bull with a sore head. I rather got the impression he needed urgently to see you—alone— perhaps he wants to have his wicked way with you?'

Sarah was innocently teasing her, but the light-hearted jest set a tide of colour rising in her cheeks. Hastily she opened the door and led the way into the shadowed hall.

'Oh! Oh! It's beautiful!' Sarah's enthusiasm for the cottage swept the conversation aside. She dumped her bag hastily on the floor, exclaimed gratifyingly over the decoration, inspected the kitchen and bathroom and back garden.

She had forgotten what fun it was to have her friend around. Pulling her through to the undecorated living room she explained the colour scheme she had in mind, and how the fireplace would look once she had unblocked the old inglenook and hung polished brassware on the beams.

'Mmm, *lovely*,' Sarah said, with a sigh, and Cindy knew she was not seeing the piled packing cases and dusty floorboards with their pattern of new nails and planks, but the finished room, warm and cosy.

Supper was not what it might have been, but not bad, either. Cindy, cross with herself for not providing a proper welcome, set to to make the most of her few stores. Out of it came a surprisingly passable soufflé omelette for two stuffed with sweet peppers and corn, and served with peas and herbed pasta.

'Mmm,' said Sarah with satisfaction. 'There's a lot to be said for tins and packets.'

They drank the bottle of wine Sarah had brought, and caught up on the past month's news. Paul seemed in fine form, with a chance of promotion to department head next year. 'By then you'll be married,' Cindy said, 'with no time for your single friends stuck out in the East Anglian wilds.'

'How can you be so sure you'll be single?' Sarah asked, refilling glasses. 'With men like tonight's visitor around, anything could happen.'

Cindy flushed. 'Jake Seaton has only one thing on his mind, and it's not marriage,' she said with telltale grimness.

'Oh, this sounds interesting.'

'It isn't. He wants to build a runway so that aeroplanes will fly over the cottage.' Briefly she filled in the details. 'Only I won't let him. It was in Aunt Beth's will that I mustn't.'

'And?' Sarah prompted.

'And nothing.' She drew patterns on the table with her fork. 'It's just that he keeps trying to make me change my mind.'

There was a long silence. Hundreds of things were left unsaid, and they both knew it. Eventually Sarah said, 'Cindy, love, I'm not prying, honestly ... but sometimes things can get quite out of proportion if you bottle them up to yourself. I know, I've done it often enough. Something's troubling you. It might help to talk.'

Cindy looked up and met her friend's familiar, understanding gaze. And suddenly it was tumbling out, the whole story, right from the moment Jake had first appeared on her doorstep. Sarah listened with sympathy. Cindy did not spare herself. There was no need to go into intimate details, and Sarah had far too much tact to ask, but she did not flinch from sketching out the shaming end to last night's evening meal.

'Honestly, Sarah,' she said, 'I've never done anything like that before. I don't know what happened. He completely turned my head. I just couldn't seem to think straight. I've never behaved like that with anyone, not since I was married. And I don't even know him!'

'He sounds quite something,' Sarah said quietly. 'I'm not surprised he stormed your defences.' She looked with affection at her friend. 'Is it really so terrible to let go like that? When you were in London your defences often seemed to be so high no one could peer over the top. Some of Paul's friends were quite in awe of your ice maiden image.'

Cindy got up to make coffee. It helped to have something to do. 'But how could I have just forgotten what he really wanted from me? He only wanted some leverage on me, so he could build his runway.'

'How can you be so sure?'

'He told me. He told me he was going to get his runway.'

'But did he seem that ruthless when you were having dinner?'

She paused in front of the cooker. 'Not ruthless, no. But determined . . . and very strong . . .'

'Perhaps you aren't being fair to him. What if the runway was the last thing on his mind?'

She swallowed. She had clung to the same straw of hope—briefly. 'No.' She forced herself to look her friend in the eyes. 'He's got a girlfriend. Myra Collingdale, the film actress. I found out this afternoon in the village. With someone like that around, he wouldn't have much need to want to seduce me.' Despite all her efforts at self-control, her voice trembled as she spoke.

Sarah said, 'Cindy?'

She looked up.

'Do you think you could have fallen in love with him?'

She set the coffee pot down with shaking hands. Sarah had said it. Had voiced what she had subconsciously known all along. She had fallen in love with Jake. He had invaded her mind, her thoughts. She longed to hear his voice, to feel his arms round her again.

'It's too stupid. I don't even know him.'

'You keep saying that, but it doesn't matter. Sometimes you can meet someone and feel as if you've known them all your life.'

'But he couldn't be interested in me. And even if he was . . . he wouldn't be now. Not after how I behaved last night.' Tears were pricking at her eyes. 'He said I was selfish, and he was right.'

'And so was he,' Sarah countered crisply. 'We all of us are, at times. He must have realised how alone you were, how vulnerable.'

'*And* how I might give in to him about the runway. He just wanted to use the situation. But it was my fault. I gave him the opportunity.'

Again she felt the pressure of his lips on hers, the warmth that grew like a deep glow inside her. In the living room the telephone suddenly rang.

Sarah looked at her, then jumped up. 'I'll go.' She came back. 'It's Jake Seaton. He wants to speak to you.'

'No!'

'Cindy. He said he *had* to speak to you.'

'If it's so urgent, he can leave a message.'

He would only press her about the runway. Only now he would do it without mercy or persuasion, because he despised her and how she had behaved towards him. Sarah turned and went out. When she came back she sat down without a word.

'Did he leave a message?' she asked eventually.

'No. He asked me if you had refused to speak to him. I had to tell him the truth. Then he said he would like to speak to you, and that you would know where to contact him if you changed your mind.'

'There you are, you see,' she said bitterly.

'I don't think he meant about the runway. I think he meant about speaking to him,' Sarah said. 'He didn't sound angry, he sounded disappointed. Cindy, are you sure he's as terrible as you say he is? On the phone he sounded, well, nice.'

'Nice!' Cindy burst out with feeling. 'Jake Seaton is any number of things, but nice is not one of them!'

CHAPTER SIX

SARAH's taxi arrived promptly after lunch on Sunday—far too promptly for Cindy's taste. She waved her friend off to the station with the greatest reluctance, standing on the bottom bar of the garden gate to watch the car disappear around the bend before turning desolately inside.

The weekend had been full of warm companionship, with no further talk of Jake Seaton and his disturbing powers, but now in the silence thoughts of him crowded relentlessly back into her head.

She stood in the kitchen and could see him propped confidently against the draining board, demanding she come out with him for a meal. When she walked through to the living room she heard his voice saying urgently, 'We must get rid of these clothes'. She dared not go upstairs and face the memories that lurked in wait for her there. Flushing with shame and embarrassment she snatched up her sketching block and fled out into the more peaceful garden.

If only Jake could see her now, she thought! He was convinced that she cherished her privacy above all else, yet here she was running wildly from the loneliness of the silent cottage.

The loneliness. And the shame.

The new life she had longed to build for herself was already in tatters! Within just a few short weeks she had managed to abuse Aunt Beth's precious gift and make an utter idiot of herself by falling with a schoolgirl's abandon for the first man who had come knocking at her door!

Yet, after her disaster of a marriage she had vowed passionately that she would never make such a mistake again, never trust anyone, most especially herself.

True, she had had initial, instinctive doubts about Simon. But he had pushed them easily aside, turning her head with his charm and good looks, his authority and standing in the artistic world of which she had longed to be part.

She had thought she was madly in love with him, but would love have brought such a very bitter harvest? She could never be sure.

What she had been sure of afterwards, however, was that she would live alone and never get involved with anyone, ever again. And in London it had been easy to stick to her chosen path of isolation. No one had even tempted her.

The very first temptation to come her way had been Jake Seaton, with his gypsy looks and iron will. And she had fallen blindly and madly for this man who wanted one thing and one thing only from her, and who in return promised only heartache and unhappiness!

She was an idiot and a fool, and her only salvation lay in work! Determinedly she put out her stool and easel and settled with all the concentration she could muster to sketch the tangled border of autumn blooms which ran beneath the kitchen window.

Slowly, moment by moment, the task began to calm and absorb her. Once, she broke off briefly to run upstairs and change into shorts and a halter sun top. Despite the wind which tossed the high branches about, it was sheltered and sunny where she sat. But she was seated again in a matter of moments, and was soon so deeply absorbed in her work that the knocking at the front door did not penetrate to her until it became a loud insistent hammering.

'Oh, bother!' Impatiently she addressed the disorderly dahlias. She had invited Betty's children to play in her overgrown garden. No doubt they thought a sunny Sunday afternoon was just the time to take up her invitation.

She went through the house and pulled open the door on its renovated hinges.

'You!' she gasped in horror.

Jake stood in the doorway, an arrogant hand propped against the doorpost. At her undisguised dismay his eyes grew bleak and hard.

'I'm afraid so.'

His eyes travelled slowly over her half-clad form, lingering openly on her bare shoulders and waist. 'Why?' he asked insolently. 'Who were you expecting?'

Colour flushed to her cheeks.

'No one. What are you implying? Anyway, I told you! I never wanted to see you again!'

He levered himself upright and thrust his hands deep into the pockets of his battered flying jacket.

'I know. I could say much the same thing. But we have unfinished business. And I'm a very impatient man.'

'What do you mean?'

Instinctively she took an alarmed step backwards and put a shielding hand to the swell of her breasts.

He laughed, shortly and scornfully.

'Don't look so terrified. I'm not talking about the other night—although "unfinished" is certainly the right word for *that* unpleasant little episode. No, I'm talking about something that really matters. Something important. People's lives.' His voice was harsh with emphasis. 'I'm talking about that second runway.'

'I've told you! The answer's no!'

So she had been right all along. His sole and only interest in her was the pursuit of his own plans! She was almost shaking with anger and sick disappointment.

'And I'm being charitable enough to assume that you haven't a clue what you're saying. How can you possibly know the full facts? You've never even seen the airfield, and you don't know a single thing about flying.'

'I know all I want to!'

'But not all *I* want you to! I want you to come up to the airfield, so you can see for yourself.'

'I'm not going anywhere with you!' Her voice was

wild and her heart was pounding so furiously she could barely catch her breath. 'Now if you'll excuse me——'

His hand was at the door before she could even begin to close it. He stepped forward, holding the door, his eyes glinting with contemptuous anger. 'What's the matter? Are you scared of being proved wrong?'

'I've made my decision.'

'And now you're going to stick to it, come what may? My God, with a mind as closed as that you'll soon become every bit as crabbed and mean spirited as your old aunty.'

'How dare you! Aunt Beth wasn't mean. She was a lovely lady.'

'That's as may be—although you didn't see her in her later years, if you remember. I think you may have had a nasty shock at just how senile she had become. Anyway, I'm not here to argue about history. What I want is a fair chance to present my case. Surely you can spare me a mere half-an-hour? It's hardly very much to ask.'

'There's no point. It would just be a waste of your time.' Somehow she managed to tilt her chin and meet his eyes.

'I'll thank you not to decide how I should spend my time.' He stood foursquare in her doorway, as immovable as a rock. Her thoughts scrabbled frantically. It seemed there was no way she would be able to get him to leave.

'I haven't bothered you with the reasons behind my decision,' she said childishly. 'Why should I listen to yours?'

His stern and powerful presence made her *feel* like a child again—tiny, bare-legged and unreasonably petulant.

Slowly he folded his arms and in a parody of relaxed attentiveness leaned against the doorpost.

'Tell me,' he commanded, 'I'm all ears.'

The challenge in his eyes was unbearable, too strong to be met. She lowered her gaze and looked past him to where his white car was parked at her gate.

'You wouldn't understand.'

'No. I'm sure I wouldn't,' he said harshly. 'It's a mental block of mine, I'm afraid. I simply can't think of anything that could possibly be more important than people's lives.'

'Well, then,' she said with a firmness she did not feel, 'we'll just have to agree to disagree. And since we have nothing further to discuss——' Again she tried to shut the door.

'Oh no, you don't.' He stepped forward with firm and menacing intent. 'We're not through yet—not by a long way. I'll get you to the airfield, even if I have to use force to do so.'

His one hand propping the door was stronger than her whole weight. There was no point in struggling.

'What? Drag me kicking and screaming into your car?' She tried to inject a note of cold scorn into her voice, but only succeeded in sounding apprehensive and tremulous. A ghost of a smile seemed to pass quickly across his face.

'I might even do that,' he agreed. 'Or tuck you under my arm and carry you up there. You see, I really can't believe that any reasonable person would stick to their guns once they know the full situation. And against all the overwhelming evidence to the contrary, I still believe that deep down Cindy Passmore is a reasonable person.'

His deep voice saying her name made her heart dip as if she were on a roller coaster. She was sure he would see its wild hammerings beneath the thin cotton of her brief halter top.

His eyes challenged hers. There was iron in his gaze, strength and determination enough to move mountains. She met his look, vainly struggling to suppress the colour that deepened her cheeks. Then, because she could not breathe, she lowered her eyes. His nose was straight, his lips stubborn and firm. His shirt was open at the neck, showing muscled brown flesh. Even as she looked away she could feel his eyes still on her, tangible as a caress.

'You're insufferable,' she whispered tremulously.

There was a long silence. Then he spoke, and his voice was low and slow and mocking. 'You seemed to suffer me well enough the other night.'

Her eyes snapped up and locked with his. Instantly there flowed between them a whole complex tide of emotions—hate, involvement, fear.

'I——' she stammered. 'I *won't* come with you!'

'Why not? What frightens you so much? Are you scared of being with me?'

'No!' she cried. 'Of course not! What's there to be scared of?'

But her reply was too prompt, and he knew it. Yes, she was scared. She was scared of his eyes and his lips. His strength of will and powerful physical presence. She was scared of him and scared of herself. Scared of her overwhelming longing to fling herself against him and to feel his arms holding her close once more.

'All right, I'll come,' she agreed shakily. 'But it won't make any difference.'

There was triumph in his eyes. 'We'll see about that.'

'I have to change.'

'Don't bother. It's not a social outing.'

'I *want* to change,' she said defiantly and turned on her heel, rudely leaving him to wait at the door.

Upstairs she put on a pair of old jeans and a threadbare white shirt she usually wore to paint in. Her hair was a disorderly tumble of curls but she resisted the temptation to brush it into shining order. She would not add to his triumph by making one single concession to his company. With an enormous effort of will she did not reach for her cologne spray, but turned from her dressing table to the window.

He was patiently pacing the garden path, a strong contained figure whose face betrayed no emotion. As she watched, the heat in her sheltered garden made him remove his flying jacket and hang it casually over one shoulder.

She stood lost in the sight of him. His every

movement was lithe and carelessly graceful, betraying an absolute quiet self-confidence that took her breath away. The artist in her longed to capture his grace and strength on paper, but the woman she was had quite different desires.

She swallowed twice, trying to ease away the dryness in her throat. Then she went back down to him.

'Have you got your keys?' he asked as he pulled the front door closed behind her.

'Of course I have.'

He raised a patient eyebrow at her tone. 'Only trying to be helpful.'

'I don't need your help,' she snapped.

He led the way down the path and opened the passenger door for her to get in. Instantly her senses were assailed with the luxurious smell and feel of his powerful car, bringing back heady memories of their brief interlude of happiness together.

'It's a lovely day for a drive, anyway,' he said conversationally as he slid into his seat close beside her and started the engine.

'I *was* working.'

'I'm sorry,' he said levelly. 'I really am. But since you refused to speak to me on the telephone I could hardly know when would be convenient to call.'

'You didn't *have* to call at all,' she pointed out coldly.

He glanced at her and there was a curious intentness in his brief gaze. 'Oh, but I did,' he said, and in his voice was a tone that brooked no argument at all.

They drove in tension-filled silence, up the high-hedged lane towards the airfield. She kept her eyes rigidly on the road ahead, fighting to blank from her mind any awareness of his presence so close to her. It was a relief when he finally swung the car expertly through a white gate and pulled up on the edge of the aerodrome.

She took in the scene as the engine died. The airfield was set on a slight rise and had a feeling of space and freedom which caught instantly at her imagination.

Small aircraft, smaller than she had ever seen, were parked in neat ranks on the tarmac. There were hangars and other low buildings, and then a squat green-glassed control tower. She watched in fascination as one aeroplane bumped back over the grass towards the parking area. Another seemed to be revving its engines ready for take-off. The grass behind it was flattened into a rippling sheet of silver.

Then Jake pointed. A plane was coming in to land, travelling so slowly it almost seemed to be hanging in the air from some invisible thread. She watched, lips parted with concentration, as it came lower and lower, skimming along just above the ground until its wheels touched down as light as thistledown. It turned almost immediately off the runway and began to lumber far less elegantly over the grass.

When she turned to Jake he was watching her fascination with the hint of a smile in his eyes. As their glances met the briefest current of accord seemed to flash between them. Then it was gone.

'Creatures of flight,' he said, indicating the lumbering aeroplane. 'Not built for ground transport. Would you like to see the clubhouse?'

'No,' she said. She would have loved to, but she had no intention of letting him see her awakening interest. 'Let's stick to the matter in hand.'

'Right. Come on.' With one easy movement he was out of the car. He came round and opened her door and she stepped out, surprised at how breezy the airfield was after her own sheltered garden. She shivered and hugged her arms.

'Here, you're cold. Take my jacket.'

He reached past her and pulled it from the car.

'No. Really. I'm fine.'

'Take it,' he said firmly. 'I don't want you not listening to what I'm saying because you're shivering to death.'

'I'm OK. It was only getting out of the car that I felt a bit chilly.'

As if to mock her words a sudden gust of wind caught at her thin shirt and tossed her hair into her eyes.

'Put it on,' he insisted, holding it for her to slip her arms into it.

'It's miles too big,' she said pettishly, but somehow it was easier to give in than to fight over something so unimportant.

'I told you—it's not a social outing,' he said, but he was grinning at the sight of her. The jacket came well below her hips and the cuffs covered all but the very tips of her fingers. 'Here——' he said, stepping swiftly forward and pulling the jacket forward on to her shoulders. 'That's better. Now let's go.'

He set off on a diagonal path across the grass. She followed, her head reeling from the casual intimacy of his brief closeness. The supple leather of his jacket smelt faintly of cheroot smoke and aftershave and when she pushed her hands into its pockets her fingers encountered keys and pieces of paper. The man was infuriating in his arrogance, but she felt a deep ache inside at how little she would ever know of him and his life.

'We'll go to the far end of the field,' he said over his shoulder. 'It's the highest point. You'll get an idea of things from there.'

His pace was so fast she could barely keep up. After a moment or two she ceased trying and the gap between them lengthened. Then he turned and waited impatiently for her.

'Could we please try and behave a bit more like reasonable adults?' he said brusquely. 'I know you didn't want to come here, but since you agreed to do so, I do think you might do better than trail along behind me like some mutinous spaniel.'

Anger at the injustice of the remark set her eyes flashing. 'If you weren't rushing along like a maniac I might be able to keep up,' she snapped. 'But I don't see why I should risk a broken ankle by going along at your breakneck speed!'

'I'm sorry,' he said with cool sarcasm. 'I forgot you've only just left the big city. You're probably not used to rough walking. We'll do it your way.'

He set off again, noticeably slower. She walked beside him, silently seething.

He seemed determined to get her all wrong! First he accused her of being a spoilt little rich girl, selfishly protecting her property. Now he seemed to think she was some tender flower unused to setting foot off a paved highway. Well she wouldn't bother to argue because it simply wasn't important! What Jake Seaton thought of her was neither here nor there, especially as after today she was hardly likely to see him again! She clenched her hands in the pockets of his jacket and said nothing.

Eventually he stopped and began to point out the lie of the land.

'You see that?' He pointed at a red and white plane that was accelerating down the runway for take-off. 'When he gets into the air he'll be blown right off course. You watch. He'll veer almost over the top of us. That's what even a moderate wind can do to a light aircraft.'

She stood silently beside him, watching as the aircraft's wheels lifted. True, the small craft did fly over towards them as it climbed, but to her untutored eyes it seemed to be cutting a decisive path through the air, quite unaffected by any gusts or pockets of wind. She could not believe it was as dangerous as Jake wanted to make out.

'Look.' He pointed to the orange wind sock. 'The wind's going round to the north west. If we had a second runway we'd be using it by the end of this afternoon.'

She glanced covertly at him as he watched the manoeuvrings of a plane at the end of the runway. He looked tousled, confident and completely at home as he stood on the windswept field.

'That damn young fool Jenkins,' he said, a frown crossing his face.

'Sorry?'

He looked down at her as if he had for the moment forgotten her presence. 'Nothing, just someone fooling around. I'll have words about that later. Now then, can you see the church tower, just beyond the tall hedge over there——'

Patiently he began to explain again the logistics of another runway but the breeze took his words away from her and her head was spinning from his disturbing nearness. Standing with his feet apart, his arm out to indicate where she should look next, he was every inch the lord of his territory. The wind was getting up, tearing at his thick dark hair and flattening the cotton of his shirt against the firm planes of his chest.

With a feeling like pain she remembered reaching for him, sliding her hands around him, drawing him close. She shut her eyes, before the memories could drown her, but she was lost again in those moments of touch and closeness, desire and shame.

'Oh!' She gasped and her eyes flew open. Jake had touched her arm, to make her follow his pointing hand.

He looked across at her. 'What is it?'

'Nothing.' She flushed. 'Nothing at all.'

Slowly and deliberately he withdrew his hand from where it lay casually touching her arm. 'Excuse me,' he said sardonically, and in his eyes was a hard, mocking anger. 'I must have got carried away.'

The flush in her cheeks became a tide of deep colour. She looked down. Jake's look had told her quite plainly that he had forgotten—and forgiven—nothing.

There was a long, dreadful silence. Then Jake said formally. 'I won't keep you much longer. I just want you to come up to the control tower with me. You'll be able to see your cottage from there—and just how little you'd be affected by any flying from here.'

He set off again, at a slower pace, but silent and remote. It was as if he had lost all interest in her, even the urge to taunt and punish, and simply wanted their meeting over and done with.

She matched his pace and followed him up the tower stairs and into the control room. Two men were busy controlling the movements of the light aeroplanes as they came and went from the airfield. A splutter of muffled radio messages came from the speakers before them and the room was hung with maps, telex reports and check lists.

Jake greeted the men with a silent hand movement and indicated she should not disturb their concentration by speaking.

Despite the tumult inside her, and the chilling coldness of Jake's manner, she was gripped by this glimpse into the complicated, disciplined world of flying. She watched as a plane soared up into the air and banked in a slow turn above the village. Its movements were so elegant that she longed to reach for a pencil and paper to capture the moment, but then there was a lull in proceedings and Jake demanded her attention once again. Methodically he pointed out exactly where the runway would go, and how the flight path would only just clip the bottom of her orchard. From the height of the tower she could see not only the grounds of Rose Cottage, but also its snug roof. Unconsciously she sighed deeply. It looked so cosy, nestled down among its garden, but owning it had not proved an unalloyed pleasure. Of course the easiest thing would be to give in to Jake's relentless pressure and let him build his runway. But Aunt Beth had made her wishes quite plain and surely she had to honour them?

'Busiest Sunday for a long time,' said one of the controllers, turning to Jake. 'There's an airshow down near Cambridge this afternoon. That's why we've got all this *en route* traffic passing through.'

Jake scanned the sky with narrowed eyes. Then he reached for a pair of binoculars which stood on the main table, and trained them on a distant black speck.

'Is that Tango November coming back in?'

The controller screwed up his eyes. 'Uh huh. At least, it looks like it. Hard to tell for sure, though, with so

many aircraft about. This field's getting busier and busier.'

'Who's flying her?'

The controller flashed a quick grin at him. 'Our Miss Collingdale. She's been off on a local cross country flight. Booked out to—oh, where the hell was it, Jim?'

Jake cut in, 'Sywell. We worked out her route last night. She needs to practise her navigation.'

Last night. Cindy's eyes flew to him, but he appeared quite unaware of her.

'I don't know about that,' the controller said, 'but she's a smart little pilot, all right. She flies some of the best landings we see here, *and* she uses the radio properly—which is more than you can say for most weekend sky-drivers.'

'Yes,' Jake said, casually, 'she's extremely safety conscious.'

He raised the binoculars again, still apparently oblivious to her presence. But she knew the barb had been aimed, quite cruelly, at her. She looked at his face. His profile, outlined against the window, was expressionless. He was a very private man, she realised, who did not let many people get close to him. Although Myra Collingdale was obviously an exception, she thought sourly, especially as they seemed to spend cosy Saturday evenings doing a little route planning together!

Absurdly, her eyes began to prick with self-pity. Damn Myra Collingdale and her wretched safety-consciousness! It was not her fault that Aunt Beth had so firmly tied her hands. For two pins she would let him have his runway and be done with the whole horrible business! But she had her own code of honour, whatever anyone else might think of her, and meanwhile Jake Seaton had got it all wrong and was making her pay a price for a sin she had not committed.

Tears welled up hard and she had to blink rapidly to stop them from spilling down her cheeks. In her stomach was a sick ache she knew was jealousy.

The radio crackled incomprehensibly to life again,

after the rare moment of quiet in the control tower. She could not understand a word that was said. This was Jake's world, she thought. Jake and Myra's, and she had no place in it. She should never have agreed to come here this afternoon.

The next radio message was in a woman's voice. The controller picked up his microphone to answer it.

'Roger, Tango November,' he said crisply. 'Runway zero eight. Circuit left hand.' Jake kept the binoculars trained on the aircraft, watching intently. Cindy heard Myra call that she was 'downwind' and would be landing for a 'touch and go'. The jargon meant nothing, although the woman's voice was confident and crystal clear.

Jake was absorbed in watching the tiny aircraft.

'That's good,' he said, as the little aeroplane swooped in for a smooth landing, before climbing immediately off again. 'Ray,' he said to the controller, 'can you tell her I'll be back to pick her up at five.'

Ray picked up the microphone. 'Haldrome Tower to Tango November.'

'Go ahead Haldrome, Tango November.'

'Er, Tango November, I've got the boss here breathing down my neck. Says he's picking you up at five on the dot and expects you landed, signed off and ready to go. Understood, Tango November?'

There was laughter in the voice which came smartly back. 'Understood, Haldrome. Can you tell him I'll be wanting tea and a hot bath? Tango November's heater's gone dud. It's freezing up here!'

Jake smiled slightly as he lowered the binoculars. He glanced across at her and the smile vanished.

'Right?' he said briskly, 'is there anything you don't understand? I've done all the explaining I can do.'

She shook her head, sick with misery at the brief glimpse she had been granted of Jake and Myra's domestic life. The woman did not seem so much a girlfriend as a permanent fixture about the place, at least at weekends.

'Then let's go.'

They drove back to the cottage in silence. When Jake stopped the engine she began to open her car door, anxious only to escape to the relative shelter of Rose Cottage.

But Jake turned in his seat, forcing her to meet his eyes. 'Well?' he asked.

'Well what?' she replied defiantly.

'Well, did you follow everything I explained to you?'

'Yes, of course. I'm not an idiot.'

'You understand why we need that second runway?'

'I can see it would be useful.'

'Useful? My God——' He ran an impatient hand through his hair then took a deep breath and, as if addressing a very small child asked slowly, 'You did see how very little it would affect your property, didn't you?'

'Yes,' she acknowledged.

'And,' he continued slowly and emphatically, 'you agree it would hardly affect your life in any serious way.'

'Yes,' she agreed honestly. She would not be affected. It would be Aunt Beth's spirit that would rest uneasy.

'So you will give your permission.' His eyes were holding hers, willing her into submission, and what he said was a statement, not a question.

She took her courage in both hands and continued to meet his gaze, her chin lifted. 'No,' she said. 'I won't.'

His eyes darkened in cold, silent rage. She felt ravaged by his look and it took every last ounce of will not to look away.

'I don't believe what I'm hearing!' he ground out.

'I told you it would make no difference! I told you you would be wasting your time!'

'Which I obviously was! Haven't you learned anything this afternoon?' The contempt in his tone was almost worse than the anger.

'Yes. Oh yes, I certainly have!' she flashed back at him. 'The main thing I've learnt is that my very worst suspicions about you were right all along! You just want to use people for your own ends! You don't care about their feelings, or their motives or anything, just as long as you get what you want!'

She flung open the car door.

'Cindy——'

'Leave me alone Jake Seaton! I've had just about enough of your bullying self-righteousness. There's more to life than just flying, you know!'

Anger propelled her onwards, so that she flung back the restraining arm that Jake put out. She stood in the lane and turned to slam the door. A pulse of fury beat at Jake's jaw as he looked at her with stony eyes.

'For Christ's sake——'

'I've heard enough!' she shouted. 'If it wasn't for you I could have put in a good afternoon's work. Now it's too late. The light's already going.'

Instinctively he glanced at his watch.

'It's almost five o'clock,' she told him harshly. 'Time you went to pick up your girlfriend—the one who's so safety-conscious!'

With one movement she slammed the car door and turned up the path. Her heart was hammering so loudly she could hear blood drumming in her ears. Who did he think he was, this Jake Seaton! And what right did he have to come walking into her life, making demands she could not meet! Accusing her of all manner of crimes when she did not comply with his wishes!

On shaky legs she reached the front door and fished down into her bag for her keys. There was something in the way, some bulky material ... With horror she looked down and saw a battered cuff of leather dwarfing her fingers. She had walked off not only in anger, but also in Jake's flying jacket!

She stood stock still.

If she carried on into the cottage she would have to see him again to return it. Or else he would come barging round with a ready-made excuse for resuming the battle of the runway.

But she could not turn back now. She was not even sure he was still there. Hesitantly she turned back towards the lane.

Jake was not only still there but had got out of his seat and was leaning against the car bonnet regarding her.

Their eyes met. She looked down at the jacket and doubtfully back at him. There was only one thing to do, although it hurt her pride badly to do it.

She put her bag on the step and pulled off the jacket. Eyes down, she folded it neatly over her arm and marched back up the path. When she reached Jake she proferred her arm. He took the jacket from it.

'Thank you,' he said in a deep voice. Her eyes went up to him. The anger had gone from his face and in its place was an expression almost like tender amusement. She swallowed away the dryness in her throat.

'Thank you,' she managed to get out, 'for lending it to me.'

His mouth quirked slightly and there were smile creases at his eyes.

'It was,' he said, 'oddly, considering the circumstances, my pleasure.'

Then as she stood dumbfounded, he bowed a little, got into his car and roared off.

CHAPTER SEVEN

THE days passed but Jake neither telephoned or called. Finally, it seemed, he had accepted that she would not change her mind. The battle was over.

She did not know whether to feel glad or sorry and sank her confusion in a whirlwind of work. Slowly the cottage took shape around her. She painted the living room white and unrolled her few bright rugs on the boards which she had laboriously polished. Everything looked fresh and welcoming, but the peace which Rose Cottage had originally promised was elusive.

Only in painting did she find some happiness, and for long hours at a stretch she worked with total absorption at canvasses which showed the wonderful windswept East Anglian skies. Ever since her afternoon at the airfield she had found herself looking up to monitor the ever-changing panoramas of cloud and sunshine, often pausing in her work to watch the aircraft which scythed through the air to and from Haldrome.

But always, when she finally laid her brushes down, her spirits sank as low as her ever-diminishing funds.

Betty noticed it. 'You haven't been up to the village much lately,' she said to Cindy one afternoon in the shop.

'No—I've been rather busy.'

It was only half true. She was increasingly reluctant to walk up the lane, ever since the afternoon she had had to double back in her tracks until Jake's powerful car pulled away from the shop.

Betty said: 'I've been thinking, Cindy. It can't be good for you to spend so much time alone. I know you want to get on with your painting, but don't you think you ought to get out a bit more? You could take up an evening class, or something. There's a bus to the technical college most evenings.'

'It's not an evening class I need. It's a job. My money's running out fast.' Cindy smiled ruefully at her friend. 'When I first came here I thought I might be able to survive to the New Year. But that was before I found out how expensive paint and wallpaper can be! I've been looking in the paper, but I haven't got the transport to get to anything outside the village.'

Betty frowned. 'That really is a problem. There's only Dutton's, the turkey farm, and they've been laying people off lately. And Haldrome.' She laughed. 'I don't suppose you can teach people to fly?'

'Teach people to fly?' said a clear, cheerful female voice behind her. 'There's nothing to it. They just like to pretend it's difficult.'

Cindy whipped round. Coming into the shop was Myra Collingdale, casually chic in a black jacket and red tailored trousers. Her dark hair was drawn back into a heavy chignon at the nape of her neck, around which was knotted a dove grey silk scarf, and her famous face was as flawless in real life as it was on the screen.

She could not help but stare. By comparison her own cream sweater and tan cords looked timidly rustic.

Myra's smile was full and generous. She looked from Cindy to Betty. 'I'm terribly sorry. It was rude of me to interrupt like that. Only I couldn't help hearing what you were saying.'

She stood back, as if to take her place in the queue, but Betty said: 'We were only gossiping. What can I get you?'

Myra asked for some cigarettes. 'Every year I resolve to give them up,' she said, pulling an apologetic face, 'but it never seems to happen.'

'It took me three goes,' Betty said. 'It was only when I saw the children imitating me with their crayons that I finally stopped.'

Cindy could not take her eyes from the beautiful

actress. Her mascaraed lashes were long and thick, and her wide mouth met over perfect teeth. There was an air of luxuriant sensuousness about her, although the trimness of her naturally full figure spoke of a firmly disciplined will.

Myra laughed. 'Maybe that's the answer. I should have a family—then I'd give up!'

She felt suddenly sick. A family would mean Jake's children! And suppose that *should* happen—how could she bear to go on living in the same village?

She turned aside and began to look through Betty's rack of magazines. Was solitude making her as strange as Aunt Beth had obviously become? She shut her eyes tightly for a moment. The thought of her aunt's ill health was distinctly unsettling. There was no earthly reason to think that Myra was serious, and yet these days her thoughts seemed to gallop off down gloomy byways at the slightest trigger. Not since the dark days after Simon's death had she felt so utterly depressed.

Betty said, laughing, 'That and a lot more, unfortunately. Freedom, foreign holidays, films . . .'

'Mmm.' Myra zipped shut her expensive black shoulder bag. 'You make it sound like a prison sentence. But I don't believe a word of it! Not after seeing how much Geoff loves having the children up at Haldrome with him.'

'I hope they don't get in the way,' Betty said anxiously. 'Geoff usually keeps them in good order, but if he's busy with something . . .'

'Don't worry. They always seem perfectly behaved. Anyway, we all have to toe the line up there or we have Jake Seaton down on us like a ton of bricks, and that's no joke for anyone!' Myra laughed, belying her words.

'You can say that again,' Betty said with feeling. 'Geoff's worked for him for years, but one sharp word from the boss still puts him in a bad mood for days.'

'Ah well,' Myra said, heading for the door, 'it's a devastating combination—all that male arrogance plus a nice healthy dose of antipodean bluntness. Why we all put up with it I'll never know! Bye now!' She looked from Betty to Cindy.

Betty said, 'Bye.'

Cindy turned and found herself meeting Myra's eyes. 'Goodbye,' she said. Myra went out. Cindy turned to watch her departing back and as she did so Myra also turned and the two women's glances snagged with unsettling intensity.

Cindy turned quickly back to Betty. 'I didn't know you knew her?'

'I don't, really. But Geoff was in the shop when she came the other Saturday and he introduced us. She's nice, isn't she? For someone as well known as that, I mean. She's sort of ordinary—easy to talk to.'

'She's stunning,' Cindy said, and she could not keep the envy from her voice. 'Her profile looks as if it's been moulded in marble and her eyes are incredible. You hardly ever see that very pale blue with dark lashes.'

Betty began to replenish the sweet counter. 'Oh, I don't know,' she said idly. 'I think she looks better in films than in real life. There's something almost *too* perfect about her, as if she's all china and glass and not quite human.'

'Here, let me help.' Cindy took a handful of fudge bars from Betty and began to stack them on the counter. The cosy shop and Betty's homely chatter were some small protection from the sick ache of jealousy that threatened to overwhelm her, now that Myra Collingdale had become so startlingly real. But she could not let the subject drop. 'I think she looks *very* human,' she said. 'She's sensual, like a cat.'

It took no effort at all to imagine Myra stretched languidly on a fur-covered bed, tossing back her glossy hair and reaching out for her man—She blinked twice, very rapidly, then began to read the wrapper of the fudge bar in her hand.

'Pure sugar,' Betty said, seeing what she was doing. 'Terrible for the teeth. I ration the children to one bar a week.' She stooped down and struggled to lift a cardboard box from the floor. 'If you're not in any hurry, do you think you could give me a quick hand with these?'

Together they stacked pyramids of cat food and vegetable soup. It gave her pleasure to make artistic displays with the tins, and for a moment or two Myra faded from her mind.

'Anyway,' Betty said, breaking into her concentration, 'you ask Geoff about Myra. He'll tell you what he told me—that *you're* the real smasher around here!'

'Me!' She dropped a tin in surprise and laughed in astonished embarrassment.

'Yes, you. Why not? I mean look at you—lovely auburn hair, green eyes, that perfect little figure——'

'Stop it, Betty. I'm nothing out of the ordinary.' Since the days of Simon she had hardly thought about her looks at all.

Betty snorted. 'Ordinary? Nonsense. What puzzles me is why you're still footlose and fancy free.'

She stopped what she was doing, a tin held in each hand. She took a deep breath and turned troubled eyes on her friend. 'I'm not. At least, not in the way you mean. I was married—my husband was killed in a car crash.'

Betty's eyes widened, then concern crossed her kindly features.

'Oh, you poor love!'

'It was quite a long time ago now,' she said hastily. 'And the marriage wasn't as good as it perhaps might have been, so please don't feel too sorry for me. Only I thought you ought to know,' she finished lamely. She hated having to tell people about Simon, but it seemed only fair not to mislead her new friend. She bent her head and busied herself among the soup tins. It was odd, she thought, that the only person she had felt easy talking about Simon to had been Jake Seaton. That night they had had dinner together she had almost been tempted to pour out the full, terrible story.

Betty said quietly, 'Don't worry, Cindy, I promise I

won't start asking lots of uncomfortable questions
about things that happened in the past. I just hope
you're not planning to hide away in Rose Cottage for
the rest of your life. It doesn't do to let past problems
get in the way of the present. And Geoff's right—you
are a smasher. It would be a shame to keep those good
looks of yours to yourself.'

Betty's kind words warmed her. She looked up,
pulling down the corners of her mouth into an ironic
grin. 'The only plans I've got at the moment, Betty, are
to find some way of keeping my head above water.
Beyond that, the future can take care of itself.'

'Well, if I hear of anything, I'll let you know,' Betty
promised.

She couldn't help but dwell on Betty's words over the
next few days. She had always known, objectively, that
her looks would pass muster. Her features were regular
and even and her hair had a healthy sheen. But Simon
had never been one for compliments, and next to his
blond willowyness she had felt almost insignificant.

Since then she had spent very little time dwelling on
her appearance. She enjoyed buying clothes, when she
could scrape together enough cash to afford them, but
she chose them for herself, to please her artist's sense of
colour and design. She had bothered little about how
she looked to others, and had most certainly never
considered herself, in Geoff's words, 'a smasher'.

She grinned as she hung curtains in the living room.
It was nice of Geoff to say such flattering things about
her. But then the village boasted little in the way of
females under fifty, and presumably life up at
Haldrome was a mainly male one, so he would have
little to compare her to. Except, of course, Myra
Collingdale. Her smile faded as she saw in her mind's
eye the woman's vibrant beauty. A homely man like
Geoff might well be almost frightened by such a
woman, and being frightened, would not want to admit
to being attracted to her. But a man like Jake, so
completely sure of himself, would feel no such qualms.

The telephone rang, interrupting her unpleasant thoughts. It was Betty.

'You know, I was joking about you working at Haldrome the other day,' she said, 'but Geoff says the club is looking for someone to manage the reception desk. It would be just the thing for you. The money would be good, and it would be fun. You'd meet lots of people.'

'No! I couldn't!' Her voice was sharp enough to prompt Betty to ask curiously. 'Why ever not?'

'I—don't know anything about flying. I wouldn't know what to do.'

'You'd only have to book lessons, answer the phone, take the money. You could do it blindfolded. Geoff reckons you'd be just right. In fact he's already suggested you to Charlie.'

'Charlie?'

'Charlie Yeats. The Chief Flying Instructor. He runs the club.'

'I thought Jake Seaton did that.'

'Not really. He doesn't get involved in the day-to-day stuff. Charlie said he'd like to see you. Do go and have a word with him, Cindy, he's a dear, and I'm sure the job would suit you down to the ground.'

'Ugh. That's an awful pun.'

'Pun?'

'Flying club . . . down to the ground.'

'Oh I see!' Betty laughed merrily. When she stopped she said, 'Will you go then? Just for my sake?'

'All right then,' she agreed reluctantly. 'But I can't promise I'll want the job.' To say the least, she thought, replacing the receiver. The last thing she wanted was a job right under Jake's nose . . . or was it? Somewhere deep beneath her ribs a knock of excited fear started up at the thought of seeing him again.

It was a crisp, almost frosty morning and her breath hung in clouds on the still air as she walked up to Haldrome the next day. A buzz of engines announced that business was underway, and she stood watching as a little plane came in to land then, without stopping, took off again, wobbling slightly as it climbed.

She had steeled herself to meet Jake, but there was no sign of his white car by any of the hangars, or outside the clubhouse. With relief tinged with disappointment she let out her breath and pushed open the door.

Inside it was warm, and there was a homely smell of coffee. A large lesson timetable hung on one wall, and a noticeboard holding a variety of unfathomable messages. Battered chairs were grouped around a low table scattered with flying magazines.

'Can I help you?' A young blond man in a dark blue flying suit wandered out from the back.

'I'm looking for Charlie Yeats.'

The man went to a speaker on the wall and fiddled with a knob, turning up a crackling conversation between an aeroplane and a controller.

'Alpha Echo downwind.'

'Roger Alpha Echo. Two ahead of you in the circuit. Report downwind.'

'Alpha Echo.'

'He's flying,' the young man said, turning down the sound. 'Was it a trial lesson you wanted? I'm free. I could take you up. I'm Alan Jenkins, one of the instructors.' He looked at her warmly and raised an eyebrow.

'No—I've come about a job—the desk——' She indicated the reception desk which stood empty.

'Oh, I *see*.' He looked at her with even closer interest. 'Hey, things could be looking up at the Haldrome Flying Club! Would you like a cup of coffee? Charlie'll be down shortly.'

'Thank you, that would be lovely.'

When it came she cupped her hands around the mug, warming them.

'You haven't walked up here, have you?' Alan asked. 'I didn't know people still used such primitive forms of transport. Why didn't you drive?'

'I don't have a car.'

'You don't have——' He clapped his hand to his head. 'I can hardly believe it. You mean you don't have a car *at the moment*?'

She laughed at his expression of exaggerated disbelief. 'No, I mean I don't have a car. I don't drive.'

'Don't drive?' He shook his head. 'You do know that this is the twentieth century?'

'Oh yes. Only driving lessons cost money—and I don't have any. That's why I'm here.'

'For driving lessons?'

'No, money.'

'Well, you never know your luck. That's my old Morgan out there——' He pointed through the window at an ancient sports car. 'Perhaps you'll be able to kill two birds with one stone. But you'll have to be nice to me, and never book me in for late lessons on a Saturday.'

He winked at her, then turned to watch a sleek Rover pull up outside the clubhouse.

'Oh God, James Wilkinson. He's one of mine. Thinks you fly an aeroplane the same way you drive a tank.' He pulled a face. 'Do you know, he's done twenty hours flying, and he *still* hasn't gone solo. Between you and me, I don't think he ever will.'

The man came in beaming broadly, and called, 'Right then, Alan. Let's see if we can crack it this time.' Alan scribbled something on a check sheet and ushered the man out, pulling a swift face at her behind his back. She was still smiling when the door opened and a friendly looking man in a rumpled sweater and trousers came in.

'Hello, lass. You must be Geoff and Betty's friend?'

'Cindy Passmore,' she said shyly, putting out a hand.

'Charlie Yeats.' His grip was firm and friendly.

Half an hour and another cup of coffee later, she was sure she wanted the job. The flying club had an atmosphere all its own, with its own language and regulations, and she found herself longing to get to know more about what went on. It was such a contrast to her solitary life in the cottage.

Charlie Yeats was equally sure he wanted her, and offered her the job on the spot. 'I can see you've got a good head on you, and that's what counts up here. That and being able to get on well with all types.'

'Mr Yeats——'

'Better call me Charlie, everyone does.'

'Charlie—are you in charge here?'

'I'm responsible for all the flying, if that's what you mean. It's not my club. It belongs to Jake Seaton. You've probably heard of him. You'll see him around right enough, but he doesn't have all that much to do with the pupils. He's mainly busy with his aeroplane. That's when he's here. A lot of the time he's off flying abroad. America. All over.'

She swallowed and looked directly at the older man. 'I would like the job very much, but there is a problem. I met Jake Seaton when I first came to live here and— well, we didn't get on very well. There's an issue on which we didn't agree. I wouldn't want to take this job without him being consulted first, because he might very well not want to employ me.'

'I see,' Charlie said, a little uncertainly. 'Well, that's all right by me. I'll give him a ring when he gets back tonight. But I'm sure there'll be no problem. Jake's not one to bear anyone a grudge, and he's anxious to get a good person in to run the show.' He smiled at her anxious face. 'Don't you worry, young Cindy. It probably isn't something he even remembers.'

But he was wrong about that, she could tell the minute she heard Jake's voice. The telephone rang as she was out in the garden trying to force a spade through the close-packed earth of the vegetable garden.

'Hello?'

'Cindy. It's Jake.'

'Oh!'

There was a cool pause.

'Are you all right? You sound breathless.'

'I—I was busy digging the garden.'

'I see. Charlie tells me you want to work at the flying club.'

'Only if you don't mind.' She had to clutch the telephone with both hands, she was shaking so much. Yet his voice sounded impersonal and businesslike.

'Why should I mind? If my Chief Flying Instructor wants you there, I'm perfectly happy to trust his judgment.'

'Thank you—I won't let you down.' Why had she said that?

'It's not me you need to worry about. Charlie will be your boss.'

'Yes.'

'I only hope the experience makes you realise exactly why I need to build that other runway. Good night Cindy.' The phone went dead.

Over the next few days the anticipation of working at Haldrome gave her butterflies in her stomach. It was not the job, but the thought of seeing Jake again. She longed to see him, but she had to acknowledge sadly that it would be the best thing all round if he never set foot in the clubhouse.

Yet he was there the first morning when she arrived prompt at eight-thirty. He was the only person around and she stopped short in the doorway when she saw him lounging in a chair, his feet on a low table and a newspaper folded in front of him.

He was every bit as carelessly, powerfully handsome as she remembered, and her knees shook with the shock of his presence. But he greeted her coolly and his eyes on her were dark, betraying nothing.

'Good morning, Cindy. There's the desk. I'm sure Charlie will show you your duties when he arrives. Meanwhile there are plenty of mugs in the back, if you want to make yourself coffee.'

'Thank you—can I get you one?'

He smiled ironically. 'Such service.' He seemed about to add something further, then stopped. She flushed, sure he had been about to make some cruel comment, and left quickly for the back room. Then she heard Charlie come in.

'Good Lord, Jake! What the hell are you doing here? And so early? I thought you were off to France today?'

'Not France, only Jersey. For some reason I found myself up and about rather early this morning so I came on over. Geoff should be here soon. He's following me over in the Aiglon.' There was some technical talk then, that she did not understand, but when the kettle boiled she went out and said hello to Charlie, and offered to make him coffee.

Charlie winked at Jake. 'This girl's got her priorities right.'

'Oh, I don't know about that,' Jake said coolly. His eyes rested on her all the time, hostile and assessing, but she forced herself to toss back her hair and act normally. Luckily, she had dressed with care for her first day in the new job, and was fairly confident she looked crisp and efficient in her safari-style shirtwaister with a bright red belt to relieve the subtle smudgy green of the cotton.

Charlie, she saw, raised a quizzical eyebrow to himself, but turned to her with reassuring friendliness and began to show her the basics of the job. It seemed straightforward enough, but it was a great relief when Jake jumped to his feet and strode out. His icily critical presence blurred all her thoughts.

Within half an hour she had learnt how to make lesson bookings, and work out the rates for hiring the different kinds of aircraft. Charlie introduced her to two young instructors, Dave and John, who welcomed her warmly. Then the pupils began to come in and soon the airfield was humming with the unfamiliar sound of engines revving up for take-off. One man, though, hung about impatiently.

Nervously she asked if she could help him.

'Had a lesson booked at nine,' the man barked. 'With Alan Jenkins. The young pup's not shown.'

'Oh,' she said doubtfully. 'Maybe I could try and get hold of him.'

'There's no need. He's coming now.' Jake had come abruptly back into the clubhouse, a dark frown on his face. He turned to the student and apologised on behalf of the club. When Alan sauntered in, Jake turned to him and said quietly: 'You've kept Mr Bryant waiting for fifteen minutes. I suggest you offer your apologies and then get into the air in double quick time. I'll speak to you later.'

Alan, flushing with resentment, did as he was told, but not before Cindy saw him cast a look of pure hatred at Jake. She couldn't help but sympathise. She, too, had felt like that about Jake Seaton! Now she busied herself looking through the filing system until the door closed on the three of them, and she was thankfully alone.

The day was long, but full of interest. For whole stretches of time she even managed to put Jake's distant coolness from her mind. By five o'clock, when the busy aircraft were taxied back to the hangars, the mysterious new world of flying was finally beginning to make some sense.

'Phew,' said Alan, perching on the desk beside her to write up his day's logbook, 'this place is a real sweatshop. Still, that's another five hours under the belt.'

'Five hours down, another four hundred and fifty-five to go,' Dave joked.

'We have to get seven hundred hours flying experience before we can train for a commercial pilot's licence,' John explained to her. 'It's such a sweat that we all keep tabs on each other's totals.'

'How about a drink chaps? Cindy? Come and celebrate your new job?' Alan's eyes rested on her as she bent over the day's accounts. 'We usually go down to The Bull. I'll give you a lift in the Morgan.'

'No, you won't, I'm afraid. I want you to stay behind while I have a word with you.' Her head shot up. Jake had come into the clubhouse unnoticed. He gave her a quick look, then came round beside her to throw his leather flying jacket carelessly over a chair.

'Leave that,' he ordered her. 'No doubt it's been a tough day for you, learning the ropes.' His words might have been kindly, were it not for the set of his face. 'I'm sure the lads will be only too happy to drive you to the pub—and I would like some *privacy*.' His mouth quirked in cold irony, as he laid subtle stress on the last word, and colour rose instantly to her cheeks. It was a relief to put down her pen and follow Dave and John outside.

In the car Dave said, 'I just don't know what's got into the boss lately. He seems in a permanent bad mood.'

'It's pretty rare for him to be in and out of the clubhouse like that,' John said, puzzled. 'He must have really put his skates on to get back from Jersey so early, although there was a good tail wind for him ... Mind you, Alan's pushing his luck. He'll really cop it one day, if he carries on like this.'

'With Jake in the mood he's been in lately, he won't have the chance. He'll be out on his ear before too long.'

John turned to her. 'What do you make of our lord and master?'

'He—he seems——' She laughed to cover her confusion. 'I don't know. I hardly know him.'

'Haven't you fallen madly in love with him? Most women who set foot in the club do—which is bad luck for them since nothing comes between him and his flying.'

Dave joked, 'Myra Collingdale has—literally. I stumbled across a very steamy little scene between the two of them a few weeks back. I never imagined you could be so athletic in the cockpit of a Cherokee!'

'You don't mean they were——' John looked across. 'Oh, you're making it up!'

Dave grinned. 'Well—a bit. Jake was trying to show

her the navaids. Navigational aids,' he explained to
Cindy. 'But our Miss Collingdale didn't seem to be in
the mood for serious study. One way and another she
seemed to manage to distract him fairly thoroughly.
Things were just getting *really* interesting when up
popped yours truly over the wing, asking brightly if
anyone had seen my headset. The look Jake gave me
made me think I might as well pack my bags and go.
Not that the lady in question seemed to mind. She just
giggled.'

John guffawed lecherously. 'I'd show her my navaids
any time she cared to look at them! She really is
something. Imagine having a figure like that—*and* being
a good pilot as well.'

'But she's had plenty of special instruction. From the
supremo himself.' Dave screwed round in his seat to
look at her in the back of the car. 'Hey, we'll have to fix
up some lessons for you, Cindy. Then you'll know what
it's really all about.'

She smiled tightly. If Myra Collingdale could do it,
she was sure she could. But she wasn't going to get into
a pointless rivalry. It was quite obvious where Jake's
affections lay. Anyway, she had seen Myra Collingdale
in the flesh, and knew she hadn't a hope against her
pouting, seductive lips and flashing eyes.

'No thanks,' she said. 'I'll keep my feet on the
ground.'

'Well, let us know if you want to go up for a look,'
John said. 'On a clear day the view's really something.
You can see for miles along the coast. It's beautiful.
You have to see it to understand what makes us flying
types tick.'

CHAPTER EIGHT

WITHIN just a week she had become a valued member of the team. She had her own key to the clubhouse and it became her habit to walk up the lane early, and have coffee ready and waiting by the time cars started to pull up. The administration of the club ran smoothly, so she had plenty of time to soothe nervous pupils with a sympathetic word, or sew on stray buttons for the young instructors who were adept at handling aeroplanes, but hopeless at more mundane tasks.

Charlie explained what the technical jargon of flying meant. He taught her to identify the different kinds of aeroplane, and to know when a landing was smoothly controlled, or when an aircraft was thumped down heavily on the tarmac by an inexperienced pupil. Jake was nowhere to be seen. Then she learned from Dave that he had left for an aerobatic competition in Australia and she was able to relax more fully into the job.

Late one afternoon, when John and Dave were out flying with pupils, and Charlie was over in one of the hangars, Alan came and perched on her desk.

'What's this? Young Cinders left alone while everyone else has gone to the ball?'

'Ssh—I must check how many hours Bravo November has flown today. The log sheet is out. One of the pupils must have filled it in wrongly.'

She totted up a column of figures, and sighed with satisfaction when it finally came right.

Alan said, 'What are you doing now?'

'Nothing special. I was going to order some more brochures from the printers.'

'Leave it, it's not urgent. I want you to come flying with me.'

91

'Oh!' Her eyes widened.

'I was talking to Charlie about it. He agreed it was crazy to have someone working here who had never been up in an aircraft.'

Outside a little plane taxied back on to the tarmac apron.

'Look,' Alan said. 'Dave's landed. He can keep an eye on things here for half an hour.'

'Well——' she said doubtfully.

'Frightened?' he teased her.

'A bit,' she admitted. The idea excited and frightened her in about equal measure. 'I've never even been up in a big aeroplane.'

'You'll enjoy it. It's fun,' he assured her with conviction. 'It'll make you understand what gives people the flying bug.'

Unconsciously his words touched something inside her. Jake was as at home in the air as on the ground, but it was an experience she knew nothing about. If she went up now, it might somehow bring her a fraction closer to him, make her understand the thrill he got from his chosen life.

Once strapped into her passenger seat, though, it somehow didn't seem such a good idea. The aircraft was tiny from the inside, and very frail, with just two seats. When Alan turned on to the runway and began to accelerate for take off she thought it would shake to pieces.

Yet, magically the plane lifted into the air and became a creature of flight, climbing steadily until the large chequered fields were flung out like a map beneath them. She began to forget her fear in the beauty of the scene. Alan banked and circled, showing her the airfield. The dark strip of the runway ran diagonally across it, and the hangars were like white building blocks.

'Want to have a look at your cottage?' Alan shouted over the noise of the engine. She nodded. The plane swooped low and she could suddenly identify quite clearly Rose Cottage snuggled down among its garden and orchard.

The sight smote her with guilt. Since she had begun work at the club she had come to realise how very seriously safety precautions were taken. She knew a little more, too, about how the force and direction of the wind were all-important to these tiny craft. And now, from the air, she could see exactly why a second runway was needed, and how, if it were built, only the very furthest tip of her orchard would be anywhere near the flight path.

Jake had explained it carefully enough, but it had not seemed very real at that time. Now she could see for herself, as clearly as if someone had drawn her a diagram, and the knowledge of her refusal lay heavily on her.

Alan, enjoying himself, throttled the engine back and dived at tree height across her garden. She could see the fork stuck in the vegetable patch where she had left it, and milk bottles on her doorstep. Then at the same height he circled the village, over the pub and Betty's shop, and followed the road that led out towards the coast.

'See that there.' He pointed to a beautiful Georgian house, surrounded by fine grounds. A sweep of gravel led up to elegant front door.

'It's lovely.'

'It's the Seaton Estate. Where our beloved boss hangs out.'

'Oh!' She studied the peaceful manor house with new interest, but it was deserted, the lower windows shuttered.

'It looks rather large for just one person,' she observed, to cover her intense scrutiny.

'Oh well, he has lots of house guests. And then there's our Myra. She's more or less in permanent residence, I think. Look,' he banked and turned in a series of showy manoeuvres, 'his land goes right down to the road. And that cottage belongs to him. The couple who live in it run the house and grounds.' The ground below them seemed to swerve up, filling the windscreen, as they skimmed past the cottage chimneys.

'Alan——'

When he saw her pale face, he flew up and levelled off, so that they were buzzing gently away from the village towards the coast where miles of empty yellow sand stretched to either side.

'I had no idea it was so beautiful—so deserted,' she said, recovering.

'Haven't you been to the coast yet? We must go. We'll have a day out. One Sunday, OK?'

'Lovely,' she said absently, her eyes feasting on the flocks of seabirds that bobbed on the water below.

Landing was a little frightening, as the plane seemed to bounce alarmingly down through pockets of turbulent air, but she sensed that Alan, when he was not showing off, was a good pilot who knew what he was doing. So when they finally taxied to a halt and the engine died, she was able to assure him quite honestly that she had enjoyed her first flight. They jumped out and began to stroll together towards the clubhouse. At the door Charlie stood scanning the sky. Other figures were looking up from the hangar doorways.

'What's up?' Alan asked.

'There a PAN alert—an emergency. Someone coming in with dropping oil pressure. They've cleared everyone out of the circuit so he can come straight in.'

'Who is it?'

'I don't know. No one from here.' Charlie drew in his breath. 'I only hope he knows what he's doing. The wind's gone right round. It must be forty degrees off the runway by now.'

'That's right. We just had quite a lively landing.'

Charlie frowned. 'We should damn well have that second runway. It's the only thing wrong with this field.'

Her eyes flew to his but he was still scanning the sky. The remark had not been deliberately pointed at her, and she sensed he knew nothing of her role in the matter. But she had never before heard him swear, and she guessed he was tense with worry for the pilot in trouble.

'You're right there,' Alan said, also quartering the sky. 'Our Mr Seaton is very keen on safety measures—but not when it costs him a bob or two, it seems. If you ask me——' He broke off and pointed. 'There he is! He's too low——'

They stood in a silent row watching the aircraft striving to make the runway. Her heart felt sick with fear as she heard the engine labouring, and watched the wind blow the plane off course. One wing dropped and she clenched her hands tightly, willing it onwards, sure that the lopsided look of the tiny machine was a bad sign.

But Charlie let out his breath slowly and said, 'It's all right. He knows what he's doing. He's got his wing down into the wind, so he should be able to set it down straight on the runway. Thank God it's not some inexperienced johnny who can't handle a crosswind.'

Then the wheels were touching gently, and from the cockpit came a jaunty thumbs up from the pilot. Charlie and Alan set off towards the plane. She turned to go into the clubhouse and bumped directly into Jake.

'Oh!'

He caught her by the elbows and steadied her, but dropped his hands the very minute she had regained her balance.

'I thought you were in Australia,' she blurted out.

'Obviously,' he said cuttingly.

She looked up at him with startled eyes.

'When I got back half an hour ago the clubhouse was deserted, the safe was open, the hangar keys were lying on the desk—The club didn't employ you to go joyriding.'

'But I wasn't——' she gasped. 'Dave promised he would be there. I didn't just go off and leave everything.'

Something about his mood frightened her. He seemed more angry than she had ever seen him. A pulse of tension beat at the corner of his jaw and his brow was dark. He looked fatigued, as well, his eyes shadowed by smudges of jet lag.

'Well, he wasn't,' he rapped out, 'so next time you take it into your head to go off on a pleasure trip, you'd better think twice about it.'

'It wasn't a pleasure trip!' she countered. 'People here thought that since I was talking to students all day, I ought at least to know what flying was like.'

'Well, now that you know,' he said icily, 'I hope you'll think again about that second runway. Especially in the light of this little drama. That man could have been killed if he'd lost control in that crosswind. He was only just limping in as it was. I should think the last thing he needed was an airfield with one runway— facing the wrong way. How you can still think your peace and privacy are so important is quite beyond my understanding.'

He paused. She opened her mouth, but her throat was as dry as a desert and no sound came out.

'Who were you flying with anyway?' he demanded.

'With Alan,' she croaked out.

'Oh, Alan,' he said meaningfully. 'I *see*.'

She looked angrily at him, her temper rising to the bait of his unjust displeasure. 'No you don't!' she cried. 'You don't see anything! Only what you want to see!'

'That's as maybe,' he said dismissively. 'But if you'll excuse me, I've got better things to do than to stand here discussing the nature of reality. For one thing, I'd better go and see if that man is all right.'

Without a backward glance he strode off across the tarmac towards the plane that had just landed.

Near to tears, she went into the clubhouse. Dave was sitting at the desk.

'You didn't leave the clubhouse unattended, did you?' she gasped out urgently.

'No, of course not. Why?'

MAIL THIS CARD TO RECEIVE 4 ROMANCE NOVELS PLUS A VALUABLE GIFT

FREE

▼ Tear off and mail this card today. ▼

EXTRAS:

- OUR FREE NEWSLETTER HEART TO HEART
- OUR FREE MAGAZINE ROMANCE DIGEST
- SPECIAL-EDITION HARLEQUIN BESTSELLERS TO PREVIEW FOR TEN DAYS
- NO OBLIGATION TO BUY EVER

SAVINGS:

$1.74 OFF THE TOTAL RETAIL PRICE. PAY NOTHING MORE FOR SHIPPING AND HANDLING.

SAVINGS DATA CARD

Notice: Mail this card today to get 4 Free Harlequin Romance novels plus a FREE valuable gift. You'll get 6 brand-new Romance novels every month as they come off the presses for only $1.66 each (a savings of $0.29 off the retail price) with no extra charges for shipping and handling. You can return a shipment and cancel anytime. The 4 FREE books and valuable gift are yours to keep!

116-CIR-EAXS

(Please PRINT in ink)

☐ MS
☐ MISS
☐ MRS.

FIRST NAME _____ INITIAL _____ LAST NAME _____

ADDRESS _____ APT. _____

CITY OR TOWN _____ STATE _____ ZIP CODE _____

Offer limited to one household and not valid for present subscribers. Prices subject to change.

NOTE: IF YOU MAIL THIS CARD TODAY YOU'LL GET A SECOND MYSTERY GIFT FREE

**Mail this computerized
SAVINGS DATA CARD TODAY
to get 4 Romance Novels and a valuable gift
FREE**

RUSH
TIME SENSITIVE

Harlequin Reader Service
2504 W. Southern Avenue
Tempe, Arizona 85282

Postage will be paid by addressee

First Class   Permit No. 70   Tempe, AZ

BUSINESS REPLY CARD

NO POSTAGE
NECESSARY
IF MAILED
IN THE
UNITED STATES

'Jake's furious. He said everything was just left.'

'That's nonsense. I only nipped out for a second to get something from the car. I was never more than twenty feet away. He's just in a foul temper about something or other.'

'Who is?' asked Alan, coming through the door.

'Jake. He's been getting at Cindy for going off with you.'

'It's that PAN incident. He knows someone might have had real trouble getting in safely—why he doesn't build a second runway, instead of just getting furious, beats me.'

Cindy blushed and bent her head.

'Anyway,' Alan said cheerfully, 'the bloke's all right, although his engine's a bit of a mess. He was coming in from Amerstam, trying to get to Manchester. Luckily he's pretty experienced—he flies for a living in Holland. A Mr van der Uys.'

'That's lucky,' said Dave.

'Good,' she said dully. She felt exhausted by the tension, flayed by Jake's scorn. And what if he was right? What if she was selfishly protecting her peace of mind at the expense of other people's lives? After all, Aunt Beth was dead, and life had to go on. She had wanted to give Cindy peace of mind, but it still eluded her.

'Hey Cinders, what's up?'

'I'm all right, Alan, just a bit tired.'

'It's your flying,' Dave joked. 'She can't stand the strain!'

'Well, here's an invitation to cheer you up,' Alan said. 'Drinks at The Bull, courtesy of Mr van der Uys. He's so pleased to be alive and in one piece he wants us all to go and celebrate with him. Needless to say, I accepted on the spot!'

Through the window she saw Jake standing talking to the pilot who had just landed. The two men came into the clubhouse and Jake pointed out the back room where the Dutchman could make his necessary telephone calls in peace. As soon as the man had gone he looked at her and instinctively she tensed inside, waiting for the next onslaught of scornful criticism. Instead he said levelly, 'I hear I owe you an apology.'

'What for?' she said, incredulous.

'Charlie tells me he gave his approval for you to go off flying.'

'Yes, of course! I wouldn't have dreamt of going unless he said it was OK!'

She was dismayed to realise what a very low opinion he had of her.

'No,' he said enigmatically, 'I should have realised that. However,' he added coolly, 'I have no intention of apologising about that other matter. Every word about that holds true, and always will. It's one area where I see no reason to retract anything I've ever said to you.'

She met his gaze with difficulty, uncomfortably aware of Alan and Dave's curious glances. 'As I think I've said before,' she said shakily, 'it's an area where we'll have to agree to disagree,'

His eyes raked her face as if she was beneath contempt. Under the desk where she sat, her hands were clenched so tightly that the knuckles showed white. They were both as still as statues for a moment, facing each other, then with a brutal oath he turned and went out. With a great effort she ignored Dave's raised eyebrow to Alan, turning with trembling relief to Mr van der Uys, a small man with a pale wispy moustache, who came out from the back room beaming and saying, 'You come and drink, yes? Your boyfriend said so——'

'My boyfriend! He's not my boyfriend!' she protested, but she had to laugh at the man's undisguised happiness at being safe on *terra firma* again.

'Yes. OK. It doesn't matter. You will come?'

'I don't know——'

'But everyone is coming. Jake is taking me to find a room there. He is being very kind. And Geoff—is that his name?—he is coming also, once he has had a look at my aircraft.'

'Of course she's coming,' Alan butted in. 'I'll make sure of that.'

'Good,' the man said, wagging a plump finger. 'And don't you let me down, now. It was lonely enough up there. I don't want to be left drinking alone tonight.'

He went off in search of his damaged aircraft.

Alan said: 'You can't be a hermit all your life, Cinders. I'll give you a lift up there. About eight, all right?'

'All right. Thank you.' She wasn't sure that drinking in The Bull with Alan was how she wanted to spend this evening, or any evening, but there was something about the invitation that was impossible to resist. That something, she knew, was Jake. The more he scorned her, the more she seemed to ache to see him. And since there was a strong possibility that he might be joining in the celebrations, she was ready to put up with any amount of Alan's company to be there as well.

It was the thought of Jake that made her dress more carefully than usual, picking out from her small wardrobe a favourite dress in autumnal russets that set off the auburn sheen of her hair to perfection. She brushed her curls up into two high combs behind her ears, so that the delicate bones of her face were highlighted, and put on a rare touch of make-up.

The evening air was cool and for the first time that year she got out her high boots.

She sat on the bed and pulled them on, admiring their fine red-brown leather. They had been a present from Ahmed's mother, she remembered, in gratitude for teaching her untalented son the basics of perspective drawing. Despite her protests, the woman had insisted on whisking her off to an expensive Bond Street shop and buying them for her. It was only with the greatest difficulty that she had prevented the generous and wilful woman from restocking her entire wardrobe!

She sat thinking back to that day. Life in London seemed a million miles away now. In those days she had known nothing about flying, had never even glanced up at the big jets that droned through the city skies. In those days she had not known Jake Seaton, or anyone remotely like him. She had lived with ice in her heart, still numb with shock and dismay at Simon's untimely death.

She had trusted nothing and no one, and had never once let her guard slip. The thought that she would one day again find herself brushing colour into her cheeks and outlining her lips with red for a man, let alone a man who not only filled her with fear and desire, but who also looked at her with undisguised scorn, had been quite unthinkable.

Now she did not know what to think. She felt vulnerable again, and afraid. But excited as well. The ice in her heart was beginning to melt, she was beginning to feel again, but feeling was a frightening thing because it meant a return to pain as well as pleasure.

There was the sound of a car engine coming down the lane. She jumped up. In the mirror her eyes were alive with excitement. Then a car horn sounded peremptorily outside the cottage and the sound made her stop in her tracks, her heart plummeting.

How foolish she was being. Jake cared nothing for her, and never would. Tonight her escort was Alan, who had not even the grace and sophistication to call for her quietly at her front door. She went to the window. The car outside was not a sleek white powerful one, but Alan's rackety old Morgan. Alan stood up in the driving seat and beckoned, when he saw her figure at the window.

'Come on,' he shouted cheerfully. 'We're missing good drinking time!'

She waved and went downstairs, taking her jacket from its hook. Jake, she remembered, had helped her on with it, without a second thought. That was when he had kissed her, so lightly, that very first time——

She thrust her arms into the sleeves, wondering for the umpteenth time whether he would be there tonight.

Mr van der Uys had said Jake was taking him down to The Bull, but that did not mean he would necessarily return for the evening's celebrations. He might well have better things to do, bigger fish to fry, fish like Myra Collingdale, for example——

'Oh, for goodness sake!' she admonished herself crossly and made a supreme effort to walk down the path with a genuine smile of greeting for Alan. After all, she told herself, it was good of him to fetch her. She could easily have been left to walk up to the village alone.

'This is a rare treat for you, isn't it?' Alan asked as they drove up to the pub.

'What is? Being driven by you?' she teased him abstractedly. Only a small fraction of her mind was on the conversation. Her eyes were busy scanning the parked cars for Jake's white Alfa.

'That, of course. But I meant getting out at all. You're a bit of a home body by all accounts. Always scurrying back to the television news and a good book.'

'I haven't got a television,' she protested. 'But no, I don't go out much. There's too much to do in the cottage and I need to keep the weekends free for my painting. It suits me fine.' Alan snorted and swung the car recklessly into a narrow parking space. From the corner of her eyes she saw a gleam of white.

'They do good bar meals here,' Alan said. 'We should come and have one one night, just the two of us.'

She turned her head and saw that it was indeed Jake's car, parked at the far end of the car park.

'Mmm,' she responded vaguely. Beneath her ribs her heart was beginning to hammer insistently.

'Come on,' Alan said. He was already out of the car, waiting for her to join him. Quickly she clambered out of the low car and followed him across the gravel, her throat drying at the thought of seeing Jake again.

But he was not with the group from the airfield, gathered in one corner of the lounge. She saw that the minute she walked through the door.

'Cindy, over here!' Betty was beckoning her. She began to push her way towards the table. Alan, she noticed with annoyance, had suddenly decided to become courteous and was guiding her through the tables with a proprietorial hand on her waist.

'Isn't it marvellous,' Betty said. 'Geoff decided I needed a night out, so he's putting the children to bed for a change. He might be able to pop along later.'

Mr van der Uys got up to make room for her at the table.

'Ah, the little faun from the flying club, is it not? I am honoured.' He bowed a little from the waist and kissed the back of her hand with twinkling gallantry. His plump cheeks were red and she guessed he had been celebrating his safe delivery from the skies ever since the bar opened. 'So lovely a lady makes this unscheduled pause in my voyage more than worthwhile. Please, I will get you a drink.'

'Thank you. Er—gin and tonic, please.'

She felt like a deflated balloon. Without Jake's presence the evening had lost its point and purpose. Although his car indicated he was somewhere around, he had quite obviously elected not to join in the airfield celebration. For once she needed the kick that a stiff drink might give her.

She sat down in a chair that had been vacated for her and shrugged off her jacket. Charlie, in the next seat, winked at her and said, 'Our host is well away. I've never seen anyone quite so glad to be alive!'

'It was dangerous, wasn't it?' she asked him. 'What happened today?'

'Ah, lass. An engine losing oil will always seize up sooner or later. It was a good job he wasn't still over the North Sea—and he knows it!'

'But coming in on that runway—with a cross-wind——'

'It wasn't ideal,' Charlie agreed comfortably. He puffed on his pipe. 'But it wasn't too bad for him either. He's a real old pro. Been flying for years. A bit of a crosswind was the least of his problems.'

'Oh, I thought——' She tailed off, not knowing quite what she had been intending to say. In the light of Charlie's relaxed view of the situation, Jake's bleak anger on the airfield seemed out of all proportion. But at that stage, she reminded herself, no one had known how good a pilot was flying the distressed aeroplane.

She sat back and looked around, disappointment like a sick ache in her stomach. The Bull was a real country inn, with hunting prints on the walls and polished beech tables. The red wall lights created a welcoming glow and the quiet hubbub of conversation was soothing. Perhaps she should get away from Rose Cottage and her introspections more often, she thought. But she had no enthusiasm for the idea.

'Here you are.' Mr van der Uys was back with the drinks.

'Thank you.' She drank deeply and the clear liquid sent a welcome shock through her system.

'I wouldn't have thought that was your drink,' Charlie said.

'It isn't, really. I usually stick to wine. But tonight I felt like a change.' Or numbness, she thought bitterly, or oblivion.

'Good, good,' Mr van der Uys said. 'Drink, drink.'

'You look marvellous,' Betty said. 'I love those boots.'

The drink had revived her enough for her to lean forward and recount to Betty the story of the boots. When she looked round for her drink she saw that it had already been replenished by someone buying another round. Geoff arrived and Betty squeezed up to make room for him. Alan complained that he had been standing up all evening and no one had made room for *him*, so she obligingly moved over in her chair so that he could perch on the arm.

Mr van der Uys began to tell them how he felt when he first realised he had a problem. 'The needle dropped,' he said. 'I looked at it. I tapped the glass. I think to myself, "Those damned gauges. They are always going—how you say—up the stream".'

'Creek,' Charlie said. 'Up the creek.'

'Up the creek,' he repeated. 'I looked away. I looked back. It had gone down further. The engine was getting hot. So was I. For the first time in twenty years I began to say my prayers.'

'It's funny how the habit never leaves you,' Geoff said. 'I remember when I was flying up to Aberdeen once——' He began to tell of one of his own lucky escapes. The room seemed to be filling up, or maybe the drink was making her hot. In a moment, she thought, she would escape for a breath of air.

She looked up and Jake was at the bar, looking at her.

Her heart seemed to stop. Then it started again, hammering against her ribs as if trying to escape. She moistened her lips, but could not look away from him. He made no sign of greeting, but such a mere formality seemed unnecessary. His look was dark, intent, compulsive. She looked down, reaching for her drink to cover her shocked confusion. Why was he drinking over there on his own? Or perhaps he wasn't? Perhaps he was waiting for someone?

She looked up and he was still regarding her. A man elbowing past him to the bar spoke to him and he was compelled to turn his attention away. In that moment she took in his appearance. He wore navy cord trousers and a dark leather jacket—not his flying jacket, but a supple, expensive-looking garment, an almost perfect match for her smart London boots. She grimaced ironically to herself. Perhaps it had come from the very same exclusive London shop?

As far as she could see, he was on his own. A glass of whisky was at his elbow. As she stared at him, drinking him in, he finished his brief conversation and looked at her once again.

'Excuse me.' It was almost as if his gaze compelled her to her feet. She climbed over Alan's legs and began to walk towards him. She told herself she was going for her promised breath of air, but she knew she was being drawn hypnotically towards the man who had grown to occupy all her thoughts.

He said nothing as she walked up to him, only watched her closely.

'Why don't you join everyone else?' she burst out, the tension making her abrupt to the point of rudeness.

'I did, earlier—before you arrived. But I always think the boss rather damps down proceedings, don't you? Especially when you all look so cosy——' He nodded abruptly in the direction of the crowded group.

'It depends on the boss,' she said. The drink had emboldened her, adding to the glow of her cheeks and the sparkle in her eye.

'Well, this boss, then?'

She met his eyes. 'It depends on his mood.'

He searched her eyes for a long moment and her heart felt squeezed so tightly she barely dared breathe.

'I'm in the mood for buying you a drink. You look very lovely tonight.' There was something in his eyes, in his deep voice, almost like flirtation. She swallowed, her boldness deserting her.

'I was just going for some air.'

'Air you can get any time,' he said dismissively. 'I'm not sure how often I'll be offering you a drink—given our numerous disagreements.'

More colour flooded to her cheeks as she remembered with horrible detailed clarity just what one of those disagreements had involved.

'Well then, thank you. I'll have a tonic, please.'

'A tonic?' He raised an eyebrow. 'Is that what you've been drinking all evening? I hardly think so. There's a very becoming light in those bewitching green eyes of yours.'

His words started a deep glow inside her, a faint echo of the deeper depths he had stirred once before.

'No, but——' How could she tell him that being near him again was making her so shaky that she needed to cling on to every bit of control she could muster?

'—but you don't want to accept anything more than

what politeness dictates from me?' He shrugged, as if it were of minimal interest.

'No, it's not that—— But if that's what you think I'll have a gin and tonic.'

He turned to order, then looked back at her. 'Look, I don't want to make you drink more than you want to.'

'You couldn't,' she replied. 'If I really didn't want to, I wouldn't.'

She flushed as she realised what she had said. His mouth crooked sideways in cool irony. '*That*,' he said deliberately, 'is something I've already found out for myself.'

She stood desperately trying to master her blushes as he turned back to the bar again.

'Well,' he said in a lighter tone, when he turned back to her, 'what did you think of your first flight?'

'I enjoyed it. I didn't realise you'd be able to see so much. I could see the milk bottles on my doorstep, and the fork in the garden.'

'Ah yes, the wilderness garden. How is the solo digging marathon going?'

Last time they had talked about her garden they had also been in a country pub together. But how different things had been then. Now they had a whole complex history behind them, and one that had caused a gulf the size of the Grand Canyon to open up between them.

'That's going fine.' It was a lie. She had barely managed to turn over half a flower bed.

'And the cottage?'

'That's fine, too. It's virtually finished. It's been such a help to have the job at the club. I've been able to afford all sorts of odds and ends that I thought I'd have to wait for.'

'Like——' Jake prompted. He seemed genuinely interested.

'Oh, like a blind for the kitchen, and new door knobs and coat hooks——'

Suddenly she felt an arm on her shoulder. 'Hey, Cinders, we're going back to Geoff and Betty's for coffee.' Alan had come up to them. 'Old van der Uys has had to make his excuses and leave. He was last seen staggering off to his room singing "Tulips from Amsterdam"!'

'Oh, but I'm not sure I want to——' She could have cursed a million curses at the unwelcome intrusion. And how would Alan's uninvited familiarity seem to Jake?

She read the answer in his eyes as Alan made his way on towards the cloakroom. His expression was dark and stony. He had retreated from her, back into himself.

'Well, I'm glad to hear things are going so well for you,' he said, expressionlessly. He swallowed back his whisky. 'The trouble is, I'm sure that the cosier your nest, the less willing still you'll be to have the disturbance of that second runway—even after what you saw this afternoon!'

Contempt had crept back into his voice. Their brief moment of accord had vanished. She looked at him, hurt beyond measure at his abrupt change of manner.

'Do you have to bring that up all the time!' she burst out, bruised and angry.

'Yes.' He put his glass down hard on the bar. 'Yes, I do. What else do we have to talk about?'

She looked at him silently, with troubled eyes. Then Alan was back beside her.

'Are you coming——' he asked.

'Yes!' She turned to him with relief. 'Yes, I am! I'll just get my things.'

'Thank you for the drink,' she said to Jake, forcing her voice to sound as stony as his. He nodded, and turned away.

She threaded her way back to the table, fighting to keep tears from springing to her eyes.

'My,' Betty said, 'you two made a handsome couple at the bar. Matching boots and jacket, just like an advertisement from *Country Life*!'

'I wish the *conversation* had been a bit more handsome,' she said bitterly. 'Unfortunately Jake Seaton has a one-track mind.'

'Oh, really?' Betty said with interest. 'I didn't think he was the sort to——'

'No, I don't mean like that,' she cut in. 'It's just something about the cottage. He won't let it rest.'

'Well he's bound to be feeling a bit sour. No one likes being stood up.'

She stopped short, one arm in, one arm out of her jacket. 'What do you mean?'

'Myra Collingdale was supposed to be coming up on the evening train. He went off to meet her earlier, but while he was away she phoned here to say she'd been delayed. She said she was going to try to drive up, but if she wasn't here by ten, then not to expect her.'

'Oh.' She looked at her watch. It was a few minutes past ten. She looked to the bar. Jake had left. Earlier she had thought that maybe Jake had stayed in the pub to see her. It was a vain hope, a foolish thought. Now she could see things for what they really were. The drink he had offered her had simply been a way of filling the waiting time. Suddenly she felt wan and drained.

Geoff said, 'We'll go ahead and get the kettle on.'

Desolately she walked beside Alan to the car park. There was still a white gleam at the end of the row of cars. Jake's car was there, and he was sitting in it, smoking a cheroot.

Alan said, 'Hey, Cinders this is fun,' and threw an arm about her shoulders as they walked. She felt too tired to care. Let Jake think what he would, it made no difference.

'We must do this more often,' Alan continued. 'I'll take you out a bit. Show you around. You'll enjoy it.'

'Mmm,' she said, 'thanks.' All she knew was that she wanted to be at home, alone, burrowing back into her shell where no one could reach her, no one could make her hurt.

And that was how it started. Alan, with his boyish good looks and floppy fair hair, could be pleasant company. He was an inveterate show-off at the club, and seemed to need to challenge any authority shown to him. Jake, in particular, seemed to rile him. But Cindy charitably found his better qualities, and began to enjoy their occasional dates as a relief from her own company. In London she had had years of practice in gently fending off would-be suitors, and Alan was no problem in that respect. He was too near her own age to have acquired much confidence in the face of her skilled defensiveness, and she was able to keep their friendship on a light level.

Inevitably, though, there were problems. Like the day they took a picnic out to the coast. Alan knew a secluded spot where just a short hike across the sand dunes led to a private and sheltered beach. He led the way, carrying the picnic hamper, and she idled behind him, lost in wonder at the colours and textures of the sand, the enticing shapes of the spiky clumps of marram grass. The flying club job had left little time for painting. All she had had time for lately were some preliminary sketches of aircraft in flight, worked on in snatched moments of quiet during the day.

'Come on, day dreamer,' Alan called. He did not think her painting was anything more than a hobby, and looked petulant when she settled herself beside him and opened her sketching block.

'What's that?'

'My sketching book. All this,' she indicated the beach and sky, 'makes my fingers itch to be working.'

'Oh!' Alan flung himself irritably on his back in the sheltered hollow he had picked for them.

To appease him she said, 'Stay like that. I'll sketch you.' He was flattered. His mouth curved into a smile as his eyes closed. It was a beautiful autumn day, calm and surprisingly warm, and she guessed from his regular breathing that he had dozed as she became more absorbed in her work.

He had a slight, loose-limbed body with an unconscious grace. It looked good, spread out on the sand, the colours of his faded jeans and khaki shirt toning with the bleached dunes which curved about them. His features were pleasant, but without definition, unformed as yet. She studied him objectively, as an artist, almost forgetting he was a person, not hesitating to lean close to see exactly how a segment of hair fell back from his ear.

'Got you!'

'Oh! Let me go!' Like a snake striking, his arms had come up and encircled her, pulling her down to him. Her sketchbook went flying as her lips were brought down to his. She let him kiss her for a moment, sensing it was better that way, even though his embrace left her entirely unmoved, then struggled upright, trying to laugh it off.

'You beast. Look at my book, it's all torn.'

Alan sat up. He looked cross, but she distracted him by showing him her sketch. The bad moment passed. They went for a walk along the beach, then sat and ate their picnic lunch. Alan had wrapped a bottle of white wine in a soaked napkin and it was deliciously cool and heady.

'Mmm,' she said, lying back, 'why can't every day be like this?'

'It could.' Alan's voice was very close. She opened her eyes and saw he was settling himself beside her, very near.

'What do you mean?'

'I mean . . .' he put out a hand and lightly traced the line of her shoulder and arm, '. . . we could spend more time together. I have to ask you out four times for every acceptance.'

She shut her eyes. 'Oh Alan, please don't spoil things. We're good friends——'

'Friends,' he mimicked, and there was an edge in his voice. 'I don't know what to make of you. Is it *all* men you want to keep at a distance? Or is it just me? Or are you hoping someone better will come along?' His voice was bitter and his hand was heavy on her shoulder. 'Perhaps you could set your cap at Jake Seaton? I've seen how he looks at you sometimes. Perhaps you could make a killing there when Myra Collingdale moves over——'

'Shut up.' She opened her eyes and looked at him fiercely. 'Alan, you're being stupid. I don't want to make a killing with anyone. I just don't want to get involved.'

'Involved? Who's talking about getting involved?' His hand gripped her shoulder and there was petulant anger in his voice. 'But it gets very trying playing at Hansel and Gretel, brother and sister. You're stringing me along, Cindy, and I've had enough——'

Too late, she saw that he really meant business. She tried to struggle upright but his hands were pinning her arms to the sand. His weight came down on her, and he kissed her hard, forcing his tongue between her teeth. She tried to turn her head, but she couldn't. His body pressed close to her, excited and determined.

Perhaps she should have feigned some response to him—she wondered about that later—but she had no premonition of what her coolness would lead to. Only that when Alan finally raised his head and rolled away from her there was a venomous gleam of anger in his eyes that promised revenge for the way she had wounded his masculine pride.

It was a tense and silent drive home, and she dreaded what the atmosphere would be like in the club from now on. But her fears seemed groundless. Alan was quiet for a day or two, but his natural ebullience soon had him bouncing back to his normal confident self. Perhaps he was feeling ashamed of himself, she thought. He was as noisily flirtatious with her as ever in company, but made no move to ask her out.

The flirtatiousness, she noticed, was particularly pronounced when Jake was around. Not that he often came into the clubhouse. Her ears were constantly tuned to hear his car coming and going, but he normally strode straight to the hangars. Once she had seen him arrive with a raven-haired figure in a bright red boiler suit, and had turned quickly from the window, unable to bear the sight of Myra Collingdale walking beside him. It was early in the morning, and they had no doubt arrived together from the graceful manor at the end of the village.

When he did have cause to speak to her, his manner was icy.

'The log sheet, please,' he would snap out, and she would hand it over, not daring to meet his eyes but looking instead at the firm strong hand that had once cradled her so close . . .

On that occasion Alan had ostentatiously needed to come behind the desk to check his lesson schedule, and had put his arm about her waist possessively as she looked up what he needed to know.

'Alan, please taxi Bravo Romeo over to the hangar, as I asked you this morning,' Jake had said curtly. 'That nose wheel shimmy is getting much worse. You should have reported it last night—I see from the log you were the last person flying her.'

Alan had slammed out, and Jake had followed, not turning once to look back at her.

As the days grew more wintry there were often days when flying was impossible. She got to know the young instructors better as they hung about indoors waiting for the fog to clear, or the clouds to lift, so when, one day, Dave announced he was getting married, Cindy asked Charlie's permission to arrange a small celebration.

She bought wine and beer, and when the last pupil had left and all the business of Friday afternoon was finished, they gathered to wish him well.

She thought Jake might put in an appearance. He seemed to like Dave, and to respect his unobtrusive efficiency. But after an hour or so, when people began to drift away, she had to acknowledge that, yet again, she would be disappointed.

Alan stayed on to help her clear up, although his

stumbling actions made her realise he had drunk a good deal, and he was more of a hindrance than a help.

'Do you realise what this means to me?' he asked her.

'What?' She tipped rubbish into a cardboard carton, wanting to finish and get away. Sarah and her fiancé were coming for the weekend, and anyway she did not want to spend much time with Alan in this state.

'I'll have to find somewhere to live. Angela's moving in with Dave right away. He doesn't want a lodger anymore.' He lifted bottles, looking for leftover wine, and poured himself another drink. 'It was always meant to be temporary, anyway. When His Highness tipped me out of sleeping in here, I had to find somewhere fast.'

She remembered, suddenly, the evening she had spent with Jake. The lighted clubhouse and his anger at the open hangars.

'What about John, hasn't he got room for you?'

'No.'

'Then you'll have to find a flat or something.'

'This isn't like your London bedsit land, you know. It isn't that easy.' He threw back the wine, put down the glass and came over to where she was sorting glasses. The alcohol had obviously given him courage, because he abruptly circled her waist and pushed himself against her. His breath on her neck made shivers of dislike run down her spine.

'I've got a much better idea,' he said.

In his eyes was the same gleam of venom she had seen before, and she suddenly realised than nothing was forgotten, or forgiven. He intended to punish her, to seek his revenge. He was more dangerous than she had realised, and now she had to find a way of humouring him and soothing his ruffled pride. Otherwise who knew what punishment he would exact from her?

'Oh, what's that?' She strove to make her voice light and casual.

He still held her tight. 'I could move in with you.'

'But I don't want you—I mean, I don't want a

lodger, Alan. I'm sorry.' The very idea of him under the same roof was repugnant, but she tried to hide her distaste. 'I have to keep my spare room for friends. Of course, if I were to let it to anyone, it would be to you——'

'That needn't be a problem,' he said in slurred, insinuating tones. 'You could still have a spare room.'

'Alan, *please*.' She strove, without success, to break his hold on her. 'You don't know what you're saying.'

His eyes focused on her with difficulty. 'Oh yes I do. Of course I do. I want to live at Rose Cottage, Cindy. I've thought about it a lot. I want to see what you look like first thing in the morning, and when you're asleep at night. I want to see you coming out of the shower, all damp and wrapped up in a towel——'

'For goodness sake! You're drunk!' A deep blush spread up from her neck, but she dared not attempt to struggle free.

'So what? I'm drunk enough to know what I want. What I'm going to get.'

'No, Alan!'

She tried to push at his chest, but his clumsy lips sought hers, moving with a hot, wine-laden urgency.

'No!' She moaned, tears of wretchedness starting in her eyes.

'Stop that at once!' The main light was flicked on, flooding the room with harsh yellow. 'This is a flying club, not a cheap hotel!' Alan stumbled back. Jake, in the doorway, took in his condition with contemptuous fury. His eyes went over the litter of the party and came to rest on her with undisguised distaste. Her cheeks were flushed and her lips were reddened. Her eyes were wide with tears and fear.

He stood in the doorway like a powerful god, hands thrust into the pockets of his flying jacket, his face as hard as rock.

'Jenkins, you'd better go home and sleep it off. And serve you right if you get booked for drunken driving. You,' he raised a hand to Cindy, 'stay here.'

Alan left, flashing a drunken glance of pure hatred at

Jake, strong and icily sober.

'How dare you speak to me like that?' she said to Jake, with shaky fury.

'Dare?' he laughed shortly. 'You're my employee. I have every right to speak to you like that if I find you behaving in a manner likely to harm my business.' He walked around the room, looking about. 'Look at all this. How do you think it looks from the outside? Bottles all over the place and two of the staff locked together in some sort of passionate embrace.'

'It was not——'

'No? Are you telling me my eyes were playing tricks? The two of you were lit up by the back room light like some Soho stage show. And don't forget—I know only too well how you behave under such circumstances.'

He stepped closer, his eyes dark with anger, a throb of pulse at his throat.

'Oh! You!' Her hand came up to hit out at him. 'You know *nothing* about me! You're just arrogant enough to presume you do!'

He caught her wrist in an iron grip.

'I know enough,' he ground out. 'I know enough of what lies behind that sweet and pretty exterior to feel sorry for young Jenkins. No doubt it's his turn to get the man-teasing treatment now——'

'So what if it is?' she hissed, recklessly. 'What is it to you? My private life is my own affair.'

He moved closer. 'Oh yes. That precious privacy of yours, once again! Lucky for you I haven't told anyone here why I haven't built that second runway yet. How do you think they'd feel towards you if they knew what I know? Things wouldn't be quite so chummy then, would they?'

As ever, he went straight for her weakest point. Shaken, she lashed out blindly.

'You don't even know the truth about that! You just like to jump to the easy conclusion. Not that you'd understand, if I told you. You only care about flying, don't you? Nothing else matters to you!'

'Now who's jumping to conclusions?' he slammed back. 'But yes, as it happens, I *do* care about flying. I care about flying safely, and about people not getting killed. It might not be much, but it's a lot more than only caring about myself—which is what you seem to do!'

'Oh! You! You—arrogant——'

'Yes? Go on? I know the word you have in mind, but it just so happens that my mother and father *were* married——'

His fury was very real, very frightening. The grip on her wrist was like a manacle. Frantically she struggled against it.

'Let me go, Jake Seaton! I hate you. I wish I'd never set eyes on you.'

He tightened his grasp until she wanted to cry out in pain, and his hand came out to grip her other arm. They were standing very close, eyes blazing.

'Yes, Cindy Passmore, and I wish very much the same thing.' His voice was low, controlled, menacing. His eyes flickered across her face and down to where her chest heaved against him. His words cut her like ice, they were so full of cold contempt. She lifted tremulous eyes to his. There were tears in them, and she did not know whether they were tears of hurt or fury.

'But since I have——' he began to say, and without finishing the sentence his lips came down on hers, hard, demanding, full of passion.

Her head spun with the power of his embrace, but she forced herself to resist him. It was useless to struggle, but she stood unmoving as his arms crushed her to him.

It was a battle lost before it was started, and he seemed to know it from the first. Without hesitation his tongue parted her lips, demanding and taking until she wanted to cry out. He punished her with his passion until her arms slackened and reached out for him. There was anger in him, and he did not hide it. His lips were rough, unrelenting, and his hand forced open her blouse to take possession of her warm, tightening breast.

She bit back a cry. He was hurting her, and he knew it. But the pain was exquisite pleasure, as well, and it started a deep, spreading warmth inside her. She was lost to him, and let herself be moulded against him, aware of his need for her and welcoming the demands of his lips at her neck and throat.

When his lips went back to hers they were violent with passion and his hand crushed her breast. Then, in the middle of the turmoil, he was setting her from him, his eyes going over her thrown back head, her open blouse and dishevelled hair.

She looked stunning, alive and sensual, and he turned from her with the greatest difficulty. But she had no means of knowing that. All she felt was the coldness of his contempt, the devastation of humiliation, as he turned and walked off, saying only, 'Please don't forget to lock up when you've finished clearing up.'

Sobbing weakly she stumbled across the room to press her forehead against the cool glass of the window. It was dark, the airfield was deserted as Jake's car roared away. There was silence. Then another engine started up. The Morgan drew uncertainly away. Her humiliation was complete. Alan must have seen everything that had taken place.

CHAPTER EIGHT

SHE told no one what had happened. By the time Sarah and Paul arrived from London that evening she had had time to gather a fragile composure about her, and to be apparently absorbed in cooking a late supper of moussaka and salad.

Their cheerful company helped her through the weekend, especially as Sarah sensed immediately that Jake Seaton was not a subject she wished to discuss. It only arose once on the first night, when she was describing her job to them.

'But isn't that the airfield you told me about before?' Sarah exclaimed, surprised. 'The one where Jake Seaton wants you to let him build a second runway?' Her eyes signalled any number of unspoken questions, but all she added was, 'I'm surprised he gave you that job—after that argument——'

'It's a business arrangement. I hardly ever see him,' she said truthfully. 'And I think he hopes that working there might make me change my mind.'

'And will it?' Paul asked.

'I don't know. It bothers me a lot. I want to do the right thing—but I don't know what that is. After all, I owe Aunt Beth everything. I don't want to go against her wishes.'

'Don't do anything hasty,' Sarah advised her. 'In the end things will become plain, they always do. Problems should be slept on.'

But she wasn't sleeping well. Even though she was exhausted from her job, from running the cottage and battling with the garden, she lay awake a long time that night before slipping into restless dreams where Jake scorned her, cars crashed terribly, and Simon's death came back to burden her with guilt.

Over the weekend Paul and Sarah banished her to her easel, while they tackled the garden. It was soothing to sit down with her paints again after so many busy weeks, and to thumb through her sketchbook wondering which of the many ideas that crammed her head to tackle first. Drawings slipped beneath her fingers—a rose in the front garden, the airfield in the early morning light. There was the picture of Alan at the beach, which she flicked over hastily, and a whole series of studies of scudding clouds. The sky was the most marvellous thing about this part of the country, and her time at the flying club had taught her to know more of its moods and colours.

So, now, when she began to block out her painting, it was a sky theme that demanded to be done. The concentration worked wonders on her battered spirit, and when Sarah popped her head in to announce that she would cook supper, she simply nodded without stopping work. Paul brought her a cup of tea as the light was going.

'That's super, full of life. What is it?'

'It's a Pitts Special, an aerobatic plane. That's why it's got those stubby little wings. And I wanted to try and capture the kind of light you get sometimes when a cold front's gone through and all the dust has been washed from the air ... You get these big billowing cumulus clouds, and crystal clear blue bits between——'

'My word, you sound quite an expert.'

She smiled and began to clean her brushes. 'Not really, but you can't help but learn a bit about what's going on.' She stopped what she was doing and recited, 'Quebec Foxtrot Echo—that's the code for the air pressure at the airfield. Quebec November Hotel—that's the regional pressure. "Downwind" means someone's flying along parallel to the runway, "finals" mean they're on the last leg of landing.'

'I'm impressed.'

'Don't be. It doesn't add up to much. I've only been

up in an aeroplane once, and then I wasn't sure I really liked it. I think I prefer being on the ground, just watching. I do a lot of sketching when I'm not busy. See——' She unpinned the sketch she was working from. 'That's the Pitts at about five hundred feet, doing a low turn to the north. I did it one morning when they were testing the engine, and going round and round the circuit——'

'The circuit?'

'The pattern the pilots fly in when they land and take-off. It's a sort of oblong, with the runway along one side.'

'And this plane is what your pupils learn on?'

'No, silly. They cost an absolute fortune. This belongs to the man who owns the club. My boss. He's the British aerobatic champion.' Despite everything a tinge of pride crept into her voice. 'Geoff Evans, the maintenance engineer at Haldrome, says he's the best in the world. I don't know about that. Sometimes he practises near here, and what he does is amazing. Everyone at the airfield downs tools to watch.'

'Watch what?' Sarah asked, coming in.

'Her boss doing his aerobatics.'

'Oh, I *see*,' Sarah said, seeing far too much for Cindy's comfort. Hastily she bent over her brushes, letting her hair hide the reddening of her cheeks. There was a pause. Then Sarah said, 'That's going to be good, you know. Really good. I don't know how I know it, but I do. It's going to be your best yet. One day we'll be proud to say we knew Cindy Passmore in her formative years!'

She walked to the club on reluctant feet on Monday, wishing the weekend could have gone on forever. She loved Rose Cottage dearly, but it seemed more alive when others besides herself inhabited it, and the familiarity of her old friends had kept her worst fears and guilts at bay.

Now she had to face up to the immediate ones, and it was obvious right away that it was not going to be easy.

Usually the airfield was deserted when she arrived, earlier than everybody else, to put the welcoming kettle on. But this morning there was a solitary car parked outside the hangar—Jake's car.

She pushed at the airfield gate, one hand on the white bars to steady herself, and swallowed back wave after wave of dry terror. The thought of seeing Jake again made her feel sick with dread. The thought of seeing him here alone, before anyone else was around, was worse than anything. He was bound to lash her with his scorn, to unleash yet again the full force of his contempt for her.

And hadn't he some right to do so? Something about him made her behave wantonly, madly, without any thought for the consequences of her actions. He had called her selfish, and he was right.

Her courage failed. She turned off the approach to the clubhouse and began to pace the perimeter of the field, hoping against hope that the powerful white car would draw away before she completed her perambulation. Very often Jake called at the airfield only briefly before flying or driving off to one of the many different occasions and locations that crowded his busy life.

From one far corner of the field she could see his house, mellow and proud in its landscaped parkland. From the opposite corner she could just see the chimneys of Rose Cottage, tucked down cosily in its fold of the countryside. Her mouth twisted. She and Jake were poles apart in every way.

Her feet slowed on the last leg of her walk, but the car remained obstinately where it was parked. She prayed fervently that Jake was in the hangar, and would stay there, not needing to come over to the clubhouse for any reason. Trying not to draw attention to her arrival, she let herself quietly into the club.

The main room was deserted and still smelled of spilled wine and stale beer from Friday's party. She grimaced and moved to open a window. As she did so a male voice made her freeze in her tracks.

'Well?' it asked.

It was Jake's deep voice, and it came from the back room. She held her breath.

A woman's voice replied. 'I got through all right. Poor lamb, it was the middle of the night. He didn't know what had hit him. He kept saying "Who?" "What?" "You what?"' The woman laughed.

The clear light voice was Myra Collingdale's. She had thought she recognised it at once, and the cheerful laughter made her sure it was the same distinctive voice she had heard in Betty's shop that afternoon.

She heard Jake laugh, and the sound went through her like a knife. He had never found much to laugh about in her presence.

'Can he make it?' Jake asked.

'He says he'll be delighted—nothing will keep him away! *And* he can stay on through New Year.'

'That's good.'

There was the noise of a kettle boiling. Myra said, 'Here, let me,' and there were sounds of coffee being made.

She stood rooted to the spot, pained beyond measure at the domestic intimacy of the scene. The couple had obviously spent the weekend together. On Friday Jake must have turned from her and gone directly back to Myra. She bit her lip in pain at the thought. For two pins she would turn and flee, pretend she had never been here, never heard the two of them together. But Myra was speaking again.

'Oh Jake, I'm so happy! Thank you so much for letting me invite him—it'll be wonderful!'

She knew she ought to make a noise, a stage cough, to show them they were not alone, but instead she edged closer, drawn by a compulsion far stronger than manners or discretion. The couple stood framed in the doorway of the next room. Jake looked not at all his usual battered self, but was immaculate and imposing in a dark city suit. A leather briefcase lay on the table behind him. Myra was also dressed for the city, in an elegant purple silk dress and high strappy shoes. Next to the briefcase was a silver fox fur jacket. Her hand was on Jake's arm and she was smiling up at him, her face quite radiant with pleasure. As she watched, Jake turned to Myra, returning her smile so that his stubborn profile was softened by good humour. Then, as she stood riveted to the scene, he reached out and took Myra by the elbows, looking down into her eyes.

'It was my pleasure,' he said. 'A very great pleasure indeed,' and he kissed her lightly on her forehead.

She turned away, her heart huge and sore with pain. This was an embrace of tenderness and affection. Yet when Jake had held her, in this very same room, it had been without a shred of warmth or even kindness. Savagery, not tenderness, had been the hallmark of their embrace. This was a quite different Jake—a man holding a woman he loved, not a woman he despised!

'Oh!'

She tried in vain to stifle the sob that rose in her throat. Blindly she turned away, stumbling into a chair as she did so.

'Ah, Cindy,' Jake said, coming forward into the room. When she managed to turn back and face him she saw a different man from the one she had watched just seconds ago. The tenderness had vanished. In its place was a stony impassiveness. He looked at her for a moment, and whatever he read in her dismayed face made him pause and swallow before speaking. Then he drew in his breath.

'There you are. I've been waiting for you to arrive. I'd like the membership figures for the past five years, please, and the total number of flying hours. I also want the costings file for runway repairs and construction.'

'Of course.'

She turned to the files, not even pausing to remove her coat. He spoke to her bent back. 'We still have to see what we can do about that second runway.'

His voice was without expression, and she schooled herself not to look up or make any sign she had heard.

Behind her she heard light steps into the room.

'I don't think you've met Myra Collingdale, have you? Myra, this is Mrs Passmore. Our receptionist.'

She was forced to look up. Myra was aglow with happiness. There was a dancing excitement about her which added a rare lustre to her screen star beauty.

'Hello,' she said and bent quickly back to her search in the filing cabinet. Never before had she felt quite so drab and homespun, so bereft.

Myra began to say, 'I've seen you before——' but Jake cut in.

'Please tell Charlie I'm in London today. I want to see what the Civil Aviation Authority has to say about a second runway here. Later Miss Collingdale and I will be lunching at Sortier's, if he needs to contact me for any reason.'

Myra clapped her hands. 'Oh Jake, how lovely! Are we celebrating? But don't you think it's a bit premature?'

She swallowed back a lump in her throat. Her heart felt as heavy as lead. Whatever Jake and Myra had to celebrate could only be desolate news for herself. And hadn't they been talking about invitations earlier? A happy event seemed indicated, but for her there would be no happiness. She looked up and met Jake's granite stare.

'I see,' she said dully.

'My,' said Jake cuttingly, 'you don't seem to have had a very good weekend. I hope you'll manage to be a little more sunny to the students.'

'I always am, aren't I?' she retorted. 'I haven't had any complaints.'

Their eyes met, and there was challenge in both their glances. Behind them the door opened in a gust of cold air and Alan walked in. His eyes went from Jake to Cindy and back again. Then he walked straight past Jake and up to Cindy. He put his arm round her and kissed her familiarly on the cheek.

'And how's my favourite girlfriend this morning?' For a moment she seethed silently, her emotions a whirlwind confusion of outrage and despair. Then the very devil seemed to rise within her. Leaning against Alan's arm she took her eyes from Jake and very deliberately flashed them up at Alan. She favoured him with a wide, warm smile. 'I'm fine, thank you—how are you?' In any other situation she might have been amused by the startled surprise on Alan's face, but now her thoughts were all for Jake.

'Alan,' said Jake abrasively, 'Geoff told me yesterday that you authorised Miles Haydon to take a plane to France today.'

'That's right.'

'He's never flown across the channel before. You know the club rules.'

'Hell, but Miles has clocked up hundreds of hours. He's got an instrument rating. He's a good pilot, steady as a rock.'

'I don't care. No one takes an aircraft across the channel without a briefing trip with an instructor first. Luckily I found out soon enough to put a stop to it.'

Alan looked at Jake with open hatred. 'How could you do that? He's had that trip planned for weeks. His girlfriend's been dying to go abroad.'

She looked from Alan to Jake. His expression was like thunder.

'Easily,' he rapped out. 'Rules are made for a purpose, and here we stick to them. How Miles Haydon chooses to impress his women is neither here nor there—and if I find you stepping out of line like this again you're fired, do you understand!'

He turned on his heel and picked up his briefcase and Myra's fur. Without a word he helped her into her jacket and opened the door. Myra, turning politely to say goodbye, raised an expressive eyebrow at Cindy, and despite everything she could not but smile ruefully in response. Briefly, out of nowhere, a current of warmth and understanding flowed between the two women. Then Myra was gone and the atmosphere in the clubhouse was as chilly as an ice box.

There was silence, then Alan spat out, 'Pig-headed bastard.'

She kept her head lowered, busy putting files back into the cabinet.

'Isn't he Cindy? You know what he's like——'

'I don't know what you mean.' She struggled to keep her voice steady. 'And it *is* a club rule about going across the channel. It's there for safety.'

'Don't you dare start lecturing me about flying,' Alan said sharply. 'And I'm sure you know exactly what I mean—I mean Friday night—I might have been drunk, but not so drunk that I couldn't take in what was before my very eyes. *And* I'll thank you not to use me as some sort of dummy in your little games—— All that eye-rolling this morning! It's pathetic! If you think you've got a hope in hell against that sort of competition——' he gestured outside to where Myra was climbing elegantly into Jake's car, 'you must be off your head——'

'Morning Alan. Morning Cindy.' Charlie breezed in through the door. She could have hugged him with tearful relief. 'What's up with Haydon this morning, Alan? Got a face like thunder and could hardly bring himself to say good morning.'

She glanced quickly at Alan's angry face, sure he was not man enough to tell Charlie the truth, and she was right. Instead of admitting his part in the episode he muttered something about 'a trip he'd planned falling through' and pushed past Charlie to the door.

Charlie turned, puzzled, then said mildly, 'Everyone seems to have got out of bed on the wrong side this morning. I hope *you're* in a good mood, Cindy?'

'A bit Mondayish,' she confessed. 'I'll make coffee, perhaps that will help.' And help her to gather the strength to get through what was obviously going to be an extremely difficult day, she thought.

As if to aggravate everyone's stretched nerves further, the weather worsened gradually throughout the morning. Clouds blew in from the west and slowly coalesced into menacing black patches. The rattling door told her the wind was getting up, and she crossed to the window to see how badly the little aircraft were getting tossed about.

At lunchtime a spatter of rain hit the panes and it grew dark enough to need the lights on. Charlie went across to the control tower and collected the latest telexed weather report.

'It doesn't look good,' he briefed the instructors. 'It's closing in all round and they're expecting it to get worse during the afternoon.'

'But it's patchy,' Alan put in. 'I was over the coast half an hour ago and it was as clear as a bell. And it's still good to the south, as well.'

As if to bear him out the sun suddenly shone brilliantly from a patch of banked cloud. The wind, still considerable, whipped the clouds away and it was, unexpectedly, a glorious afternoon.

Charlie stood at the window for a long moment, quietly puffing his pipe and watching the sky with a practised eye. Eventually he said, 'Well, I must admit it looks better now, but it's obviously changeable. That wind's not too healthy, although it's steady enough, not gusting. I think we'd all better play it by ear. Take your pupils up if it looks OK, but stick close to base. These clouds can really steam in fast when they choose to. And if in doubt—scrub it. Remember the old saying, there's old pilots and bold pilots, but no old, bold pilots.'

That afternoon showed up different temperaments at the club. Dave, steady and reliable, scrapped two lessons, turning away disappointed students. Alan carried on with his programme and logged two more flying hours. 'Don't know what's the matter with everyone. It's beautiful up there,' he said.

'Dave's pupils both needed solo practice. He didn't think it was good enough for that.'

'Rubbish. It's perfectly fine over the airfield. And it does people good to get bumped about a bit. No good them thinking flying's all one big pleasure trip.'

'Well, he's just being careful.'

'No,' said Alan, looking at her contemptuously. 'I'm careful. Dave's chicken.'

He went out again and, crossing to the window, she saw him sprinting youthfully across the tarmac. He was nothing but a boy, she thought. Full of pride and insecurity, needing to prove himself and suspicious of being laughed at.

It made him easier to understand, but the more she saw of his darker moods, the less patience she had with him. He might stack up his hours more quickly than Dave, and get to be a full-blooded commercial pilot first. But how long would he last in the job, unless he learned to control his impetuousness and aggression? Whereas Dave, she was sure, would carve out a steady, solid career for himself, and be the kind of pilot Jake would be proud to have helped on his way.

'Penny for them,' Charlie said, coming out of his office to squint again at the weather. 'Or perhaps not. It doesn't look as if they're giving you much pleasure, standing there frowning like that.'

'Oh, you made me jump! I was just seeing if it was going to stay fine.'

'Who can say?' Charlie replied phlegmatically. He looked across at the lesson chart. 'We're not very busy. That chap Saunders won't mind staying on the ground. He wants to brush up his air law.'

'Dave asked me to tell you that he'll be in the hangar all afternoon. Aileen Percival cancelled her lesson when it rained this morning. That left him clear, so he volunteered to help Geoff look at Oscar Zulu's undercarriage.'

'Good lad,' Charlie said absently. 'Is Jake over there as well, do you know?'

'Oh!' Her hand flew to her mouth and she coloured. 'I forgot. He was here early this morning and asked me to let you know that he was driving down to London, to the CAA. He was with Myra Collingdale, and said that if you needed him you could get him at Sortier's.'

'Fair enough,' said Charlie, and turned back to his office without seeming to notice her fiery cheeks.

Glumly she sat down to send out a pile of subscription reminders. It was quiet in the clubhouse. The bad weather was keeping everyone away.

But then the door opened and a young lad called Roddy Howes came in. He nodded to her before Alan bustled in after him and quickly booked him out for his lesson. The two set off towards Kilo India, a little red and white plane standing near the clubhouse. Two boys together, she thought, watching their vanishing backs. Roddy was just seventeen and dead keen to be a pilot. In rain, snow and hail he would cycle up to the airfield simply to hang around, inhaling the smell of aviation fuel and watching how things were done. His father had agreed to help him get started by paying for one lesson a week, and those sparse hours in the air were the highpoint of his life.

The afternoon passed slowly. No matter how hard she tried to concentrate on the work in hand, she found herself staring sightlessly into the distance, her head full of images of Jake and Myra. In her mind's eye she saw them lunching intimately together in elegant and stylish surroundings. The two of them laughing at some private joke. She saw Jake's dark eyes flashing, and his mouth curving into a slow smile. And she thought about his mouth, and how she had felt when he had crushed his lips so savagely and contemptuously to hers the other night . . .

'Stop it!' she admonished herself silently, and got up to switch on the light. She bent more determinedly to the task in hand, so that her hair fell in a tumble of curls before her face and she did not see Charlie come out of his office and take up a position by the window.

'Look at that!' he said, making her jump. He gesticulated with his pipe. Across the flat openness of the airfield a dark bank of cloud was rolling in. She noticed that the wind sock was blowing out almost horizontally.

'Charlie, it's got much worse! I didn't notice!'

'Mm. Lucky for us it wasn't this morning, when we were busy. There's no one up there now, is there?' He glanced at the lesson chart, then anxiously at her. 'Did Alan go out with young Howes?'

'Yes. They took Kilo India.'

'Were they doing circuits?'

'I'm sorry Charlie, I wasn't watching. But I don't think so. I think I would have noticed the noise.'

'Mmm. They'd better get back sharpish.'

'Who had?' said Dave, walking in.

'Alan,' she said.

'But he's in the hangar, talking to Geoff.'

'Good,' said Charlie quietly. 'He's hangared Kilo India then?'

'No. That's what I came over for. To ask who's got her up. Geoff thought he might as well lock up. The weather's well and truly closed in for the night.'

As one they turned their anxious eyes to Alan, as he came through the door.

He looked defensive, as if prepared for the inevitable questions.

'Did you let young Howes off solo, Alan?' Charlie asked quietly.

'Yes—it didn't seem too bad at the time. And I told him to stay within sight of the field.'

'How the hell do you expect him to do that when the cloud's coming in at seven hundred feet!'

Cindy held her breath. It was the nearest she had ever seen to Charlie losing his temper. He spoke without raising his voice, but she could tell from the way his eyes never left the sky that he was tense with worry.

'I—well, it really wasn't at all bad. He should have landed by now, anyway. He was only going to stay up for fifteen minutes,' Alan said aggressively.

'How much solo has he done?'

'About eight hours, I think.'

'And how much out of the circuit?'

'Just a couple of hours. A local cross country.'

Charlie sucked his pipe, thinking hard.

'He's lost,' he said flatly. 'He's got to be lost. And if he's gone into that cloud bank he's a gonner.'

She gasped, her eyes on Dave for an explanation.

'You can't fly in cloud unless you know how to fly on instruments alone,' he explained to her. 'You can't tell where the horizon is, and you soon lose all sense of direction.'

'Oh! Poor Roddy!'

'He isn't lost. He can't be. He's got enough sense to get down quickly when he sees it's deteriorating.' Alan's voice was defiant, but his face was pinched and white, giving her yet another pointer to the seriousness of the situation. The atmosphere was thick with tension.

'You'd better tell the tower,' Charlie said. 'If he's still in contact they might be able to guide him back on a radio bearing.'

'They'll have to be smart about it,' Dave said, eyeing the gathering clouds. 'It'll be completely locked in soon. No one will be able to land, let alone a novice flying by the seat of his pants.'

Charlie moved quickly. Cindy watched his shambling run across the tarmac. Alan followed him out and headed off to the edge of the field, where there was the best view of the whole area.

Dave picked up the phone and with quiet efficiency began to relay the necessary information to the regional distress station. Then, methodically, he began to phone round all the airfields in their particular part of eastern England.

Cindy, glad to be of use, looked up the phone numbers he asked for. With one hand Dave reached up and turned up the speaker which relayed the airfield's frequency, and as he talked on the phone she listened to the calm but urgent voice of the controller asking Kilo India to come in, please.

'It's no good,' she whispered, near to tears. 'He's not replying. Surely he would have replied by now? Something must have happened.'

'Happened to whom?'

Jake stood in the doorway, his gaze cool and incisive. Dave gave the end of the message on the telephone and turned.

'Someone's lost,' he said simply. 'Young Howes in Kilo India.'

Jake swore bitterly. 'Was it that fool——'

He looked for information from Cindy, but it was Dave who cut in. 'Alan let him go solo. But it wasn't that bad. It's closed in fast in the last twenty minutes.'

Jake swung back, his eyes narrow as he assessed the weather conditions. The draught from the open door blew his hair about, but he didn't seem to notice. Outside his white car was pulled up outside the door. Her eyes were drawn automatically to the opening passenger door. Myra Collingdale stepped out, looking oddly out of place in her thin purple silk dress on the dark and windy airfield.

'What is it? What's the matter?' she called as she tapped up to the door.

Cindy watched dully as Myra caught at Jake's arm, and he told her quickly the situation. The air of easy familiarity between them gave her a leaden pang of jealousy. But somehow it did not matter. Nothing mattered except Roddy Howes. Finding him and getting him home—if, of course, he was still alive.

'Sssh!' Dave held up a hand.

Over the radio, very faint, was a crackling answer to the air traffic controller's persistent calls.

'Was that him?' Myra asked. She looked as tense as everyone else, and an edge of sharpness tinged her beautiful features.

'I couldn't hear,' Dave said. 'It was someone.'

They listened in silence. With painstaking patience the controller asked the 'unreadable' aircraft to call again. After a long pause there was a burst of crackling static, then a breathless voice. The message was garbled, but they all heard the words 'Kilo India'.

'It's him,' Cindy breathed, flooded with relief that the young student pilot was at least still alive.

'Thank God,' Myra said, with deep feeling.

Jake without a word left the room and began to sprint across to the tower. In the clubhouse there was a tension-filled silence while they listened to the fragmented radio conversation. Kilo India was unable to tell the controller where he was.

'He's panicking,' Dave said. 'Listen to his voice.'

'Poor love,' Myra said. Cindy remembered suddenly that Myra was herself a pilot, and would understand the situation very clearly. The woman was far more than a beautiful screen star. She was an intelligent and accomplished person. A fitting partner for someone like Jake.

She stared with open fascination at the woman he must have often held in his arms, and could not dislike what she saw. Myra, quite forgetful of herself, was biting her lip with anxiety as she strained to listen to the radio. She hugged herself, as if the thin silk dress offered no protection against the bitter East Anglian wind.

Almost before she realised what she was going to say, Cindy found herself holding out a sweater. 'Would you like to put this on? I know it's the wrong colour for your dress, but it gets freezing in here when the wind's from the north.'

Myra smiled warmly at her. 'Why thank you. But don't you need it?'

Cindy looked down at her tight jeans tucked into leather knee boots and her loose-fitting cream sweater, and her cheeks warmed at her country casual appearance. 'No. I'm dressed for the weather. I'm used to it.' She met Myra's gaze shyly, then looked away, out of the window. 'I think I'll make coffee, while we wait.'

She was pouring out the milk in the back kitchen when Myra came in, frowning gravely. 'Jake's gone up,' she said directly to Cindy. 'He's just taken off in the Pitts.'

'Oh!' She gasped with shock, and the two women's glances locked in common fear. 'But the conditions must be awful. The wind's——'

'Gusting up to fifty knots,' Myra said, 'and at least thirty degrees off the runway. And the cloud's closing in fast.'

She set down the bottle of milk, which was trembling in her hand. 'He'll be in danger, won't he? Real danger?'

Myra came across and put a hand on her shoulder. 'Yes,' she said quietly. 'But he must have thought it a risk worth taking. He feels responsible for that poor lad up there, and he must think he can do something to guide him back.'

Cindy searched Myra's beautiful, anxious face, not bothering to hide her sick terror. 'He's a good pilot, isn't he?'

'One of the best,' Myra said firmly.

'Even so——' she began, falteringly.

'I know.'

They stood like that for a long moment, with hundreds of unvoiced thoughts lying between them. Then Myra dropped her hand and began to stir the mugs of coffee.

'I thought you would rather know before you went back out there,' she said. 'That's why I came through to tell you, Cindy.'

'Oh, you know my first name!'

'Why, yes, of course. Jake's told me a great deal about you. You were at art school, weren't you before you married Simon——' Abruptly she bit off her sentence, then said lightly. 'Jake says you've made a world of difference to the club atmosphere. And he's often marvelled at your energy, in doing your cottage up, all alone.'

Cindy blushed. 'Oh, I don't do that much. And friends help me at the weekends. I've—I've seen you around the airfield before,' she went on impulsively. 'And in the village shop that time. I'm glad we've met. I love the flying world, but it's a very male one. It's always nice when there are other women around.' She meant it. She could not begrudge Jake Myra, who was so warm and friendly, so beautiful and accomplished a partner for him. And all that mattered now was that he should come back safe and well.

Myra smiled. 'I'm glad we've met, too. Although from what I hear, you've never had any problems about operating in a man's world—it's quite clear that every last one of them up here is your devoted admirer.' She picked up two of the mugs and led the way out, saying over her shoulder, 'You should relax and enjoy it, my dear. Don't let one bad relationship build up your defences for life.'

Cindy followed, puzzled. Myra seemed to know so much about her, about her marriage and its aftermath. Yet Jake was no idle gossip. She was surprised he would bother to relay so much information about her to his girlfriend.

But the sight that met her eyes swept away all such speculation.

'Oh, Charlie, it's getting worse!' she gasped out, looking at the inky sky lowering across the airfield.

'Ay lass, I'm afraid it is.'

He stood at the window, jingling coins in his pocket abstractedly as he scanned the sky. Myra handed him a mug of coffee, then seated herself by the window. She was very still, nursing her coffee with both hands as if she were still freezing. Alan was pale and silent.

Cindy glanced around the anxious gathering. The mug in Myra's tense hands seemed to draw her eyes. It reminded her so vividly of all the many nights she, too, had once sat nursing an undrunk coffee, waiting for Simon to come home, hoping, praying, that he would not have whisky on his breath and harsh words on his tongue. The strange and unsettling conversation with Myra had stirred up memories which were far too vivid for comfort. They chilled her to the marrow.

At his worst Simon had been unbearably cruel. She had confided in him all her hopes and ambitions, but later he had been quick to fling them back in her face.

'How's the little *artist* tonight,' he would sneer. 'Not doing anything artistic in the kitchen, I notice!'

His moods had grown blacker the longer the marriage progressed. His way of life had become more erratic. Often he spent whole evenings away from her, coming in in the early hours, and she never dared ask where he had been.

Instead she had withdrawn from him, bowing her head when he sniped aggressively at her so that he would not see her hurt. She had shut down her feelings bit by bit, as deliberately as someone switching lights off in a room, until her inner life had become as dark as night and as petrified as a fossil.

Perhaps she had even been ill at that time—mentally ill? Perhaps such illness ran in the family? Look at poor Aunty Beth—surely she could not have been in her right mind to be so fearful of the little aeroplanes overhead?

But in that case, what about the will? And her own decision to stick to the letter of Aunt Beth's wishes? She frowned, unravelling the tangled thread of her thoughts in the tense silence of the clubhouse. If only she could talk to someone who had known her aunt in her last days.

There was someone, of course. There was Jake. Instinctively she recoiled from the thought, her heart beating fast as if from the threat of danger! Abruptly she jumped up and went to stare at the racing clouds. The sharp click of Charlie's cigarette lighter as he lit his pipe for the umpteenth time seemed to grate horribly on her strung up nerves.

Perhaps there had been a time when she could have told Jake the truth about the will and her decision. On their very first meeting she could have told him quite directly, as a fact of life.

But she had been frightened of him then. He had been just a stranger—powerful, stern and determined— and she had been sure he would scoff at such sentimental loyalty.

Now she was not so sure. Some instinct told her Jake would understand her loyalty. He would not scorn

Aunt Beth's wistful wishes. Instead he would sit down with her, quietly and in private, and slowly talk her into doing what she did not want to do.

It would be quite easy, she was certain. The doubts were already sown in her mind. They had been there ever since Betty had first mentioned her aunt's increasing oddness, and had been fuelled by everything she had seen and come to understand at the flying club.

But she could not tell him! It was nothing to do with rational arguments. It was a deep, primitive fear, that made her heart hammer and her palms sweat. If she told him about the will—if she let him get that close to her, the really private core of her being—then who knew what would happen. After all, that last time, with Simon——

A sudden gust of wind roared around the thin walls of the clubhouse and the radio burst into life with a staccato of crackling interference which made everyone start. Cindy, wound up to breaking point, jumped almost out of her chair.

It had been like that the night Simon had died. First the long tense waiting, the silence in the penthouse flat. Then the sudden noise, the police's authoritative knocking on the door, making her start in every muscle.

They had been very kind, the police. They made her sit down, and one had gone to make her tea while the older man had sat beside her on the settee and told her quietly about Simon's motorway accident.

Somehow—she never to this day knew how—she had kept her face an impassive mask. Yet behind her impervious features had been a churning cauldron of emotions—guilt and shock and relief.

Although guilt more than anything. Guilt because the accident had been all her fault. She had let her guard slip, let her emotions show, told Simon the ugly truth about her feelings, and then the worst had happened! She had caused his death as certainly as if she had taken out a gun and shot him! They should have been trying her for murder that morning, but instead the elderly policeman had held her hand and tried to encourage her to find relief in tears.

She had let her hair tumble about her face, frightened he would look into her eyes and see her guilt there, and worse, her guilty relief. Simon was dead, and that was terrible, but at the same time it meant that the prison of her penthouse marriage had burst open and she was free to resume her life again!

It was a dreadful thing to be thinking while poor Simon lay dead, and she had almost welcomed the shattering pain that had rolled over her when, hours later, she finally realised that the man she had worshipped and married, was gone for ever. With the pain had come tears, and the tears had gone on for day after day before she felt able to face the world again.

When she finally did so, it was as a changed person. It was as if something—all life and laughter—had retreated deep inside herself, protected by a thick shell of cool defensiveness; almost as if the cold fingers of Simon's terrible death had reached out and taken her own young life into their numbing grasp.

Of course many people had been kind. Solicitors and bank managers had treated her with compassion, even as they broke the news that Simon's many debts had left her nothing except the few hundred pounds in her current account. She had nodded, tight-lipped, and felt only relief that there would be no material possessions, at least, to remind her of the whole terrible episode. Old college friends telephoned with sympathy and invitations, but she had refused them all. Look what happened when you let people get close to you, she thought. Look what happens when you let them see what you're really thinking and feeling.

She stood looking out at the squally, deserted airfield, her lips clamped grimly together as she remembered those bitter times. Things had got better, much better. The selfless easy friendship of Sarah and Paul had thawed some of the chill from her soul. She could almost live as normal, provided no one

threatened to invade that shielded inner core of guilt
and hurt. But if someone came too close, asked too
many questions, made difficult demands . . .

So that was it! That was why she feared to tell Jake
the truth, feared to let him see where her true loyalties
lay. It was nothing to do with privacy, or with fear of
his scorn or his arguments. It was a deeper dread, a fear
of invasion, a fear of having to feel again, to respond,
to hurt and to be hurt.

She chewed her lip so hard that a trickle of salty
blood ran down unnoticed inside her mouth. The radio
crackled occasionally from the speaker above her head
and the tension in the tiny room was unbroken.

Life was so short, she thought. Simon had been
barely thirty when he died. If young Roddy Howes
crashed he would never even live to be grown up. And
what about herself? The past few years of her life had
been more like death than life.

Suddenly there was a voice over the radio. Her
thoughts vanished, replaced by a straining concentration
to hear the distorted words. The controller was asking
Kilo India to come in, please. His voice was very calm
and reassuring. Kilo India came in promptly, its young
student pilot's voice sounding slightly less tremulous.
The controller told him Jake was in the air searching
for him, and to keep a good watch for another plane.
He then asked the lost student to describe exactly what
he could see from where he was. The answer was
halting, interspersed by gasps as the frail aeroplane was
tossed about by turbulence. 'The cloud's bad . . . it's
getting worse. I can only see patches down below. It's
all fields . . . big fields . . .'

'Can you see a river, or any villages?'

'No. No river. I saw a village with a big white house
outside it . . . about three minutes ago.'

'Kilo India, are you maintaining your heading on
one-six-zero degrees?'

'Yes . . . I mean no . . . I'm on one-seven-zero. My
fuel's very low.'

'Don't worry. We'll get you down in time. This village
... was it big or small?'

'Small. Just a ribbon of houses on one road. Oh ...
I've just seen something. It looks like a factory. Three
red roofs and a chimney at one end. There's some
yellow lorries outside.'

In the clubhouse Charlie burst out, 'Jerrards'. The
animal feed place. It must be. He's not so far away.'

'Where is the factory,' the controller asked. 'What
direction from you?'

'In my three o'clock. About a mile or so away.'

'Stand by, Kilo India.'

In the clubhouse everyone held their breath. Then
Jake cut into the conversation, his voice deep, calm and
authoritative over the crackling radio.

'Haldrome, this is Sierra Tango. I heard all that. It
has to be Jerrards'. Tell him to turn, gently, on to one-
five-zero degrees. That'll take him away from the worst
of the cloud. If I put some steam on, I can intercept him
over Berham Market and lead him back.'

'Understood, Sierra Tango. Report your present
position.'

'Twenty miles west of you, just coming up to the
disused railway crossing at Sefton. Heading two-eight-
zero degrees at one hundred and fifty knots. Two
thousand, one hundred feet on the QNH.'

'Roger, Sierra Tango.'

In the clubhouse they listened in silence, trying to
gauge the lost student's state of mind. Everything
depended on his keeping calm, and they knew it. She
flashed a quick look round the room and caught Myra's
anxious eye.

'Good lad,' Charlie said, when he reported he was
now holding a steady course of one-five-zero degrees.
When, a few minutes later, Jake reported Kilo India in
sight, Cindy clapped her hands with relief.

'It's not over yet,' Charlie said quietly. 'They've still got
to get down, and that wind's gone round even further. I'd
give my eye teeth for a second runway, right now.'

'Couldn't they try for a straight in approach, on to the grass?' Myra asked.

'No. It's waterlogged. They'd tip over as soon as they put a wheel down.'

Cindy sat very still. There was hope for Roddy, and for Jake, but the danger was still there. There was life, and there was death. In her head an absurd pact was running over and over. Let them get down safely, she prayed to the powers that be, and they can build that runway tomorrow!

Suddenly it was all crystal clear. It seemed amazing that she could ever have thought otherwise. It was the living who mattered most, not the dead. It was Roddy Howes, and all the many students who would come after him, not the whim of poor muddled Aunt Beth who had had a long life and a good one before her befuddled end.

And for herself, too. She had been living half-alive, bound by guilt and fear to the tyranny of the past. She could see that, now, because Jake had walked into her life and stirred up feelings she had hoped to smother out of existence. He had made her want again, had made her long for human love and trust and warmth.

Not that he was offering them to her, of course. Not that she could change her defensive, life-denying habits overnight. But at least now she understood something about herself, about what she had to do. She had to learn to say Yes to life again, to take risks. And she had to learn to take her own decisions, not those made for her by the ghosts from the past.

With these thoughts came a flooding peace of mind she had not known for years. She had made her decision and it was the right one. Aunt Beth, in sound mind, would have agreed without hesitation.

She lifted her head and almost expected the sun to be shining, but instead black clouds were scudding low across the hedgerows.

In silence they watched and waited as the minutes crawled by. Eventually Charlie stabbed at the air with his pipe, pointing out distant dots. 'Here they come.' As if drawn by a single thread, the watchers crossed to the window and stood beside him. It seemed to take forever for the planes to labour in against the wind to the airfield.

'Keep that power up,' Myra murmured, as if mentally willing the inexperienced boy down. The planes lurched and dropped in a pocket of unstable air, and rain lashed across the airfield. The two craft were having to crab in almost sideways, in order not to be drifted away from the runway. Jake eventually touched down first, and almost instantly swerved aside to leave the runway clear.

'That's one plane we'll be dragging out of the mud with a tractor,' Charlie said quietly, but the relief that Jake, at least, was safe was evident in his voice. Now their eyes were pulled back to the other aircraft, swerving and wobbling towards the runway.

'Too high. Too *high*,' Myra urged, unaware she was speaking. The plane suddenly dropped fifty feet like a stone. 'Lucky he was,' said Charlie. 'Look at that wind shear.'

They held their breath. One wheel of the plane touched the runway. The other was forced down. The plane bounced into the air again and lurched violently out of control, one wing tip dipping almost to the ground.

For horrible seconds it seemed certain the plane would cartwheel to pieces. Then it was on the runway again, veering off course, but with both wheels on the ground. It ran off the tarmac at high speed, and into the soaking grass. The abrupt transition put a brake on the wheels. The nose tipped over and the propeller, splintering to a halt, stabbed deeply into the soft ground.

'Oh!' Charlie shuddered at the noise, but his shoulders relaxed as he watched Jake run up to the broken plane and pull its pilot down from the cockpit. Two figures began to run across the grass, away from the danger of explosion and fire.

'Oh!' Cindy turned away with a shudder of relief. 'Thank God! They're both safe!' Suddenly she could not stop trembling and shuddering. Jake was safe. But if anything had happened to him—or to Roddy—on landing, then it would have been her fault! Her fault in not allowing him to build that second runway. Her selfishness, in wanting peace of mind at the expense of other people's safety! Jake was right. She was the most selfish person alive!

'Cindy, what is it?' Myra asked, coming over.

'I'm all right. It's silly. It's just the relief.' But she wasn't all right. Tears were pouring down her face.

'Why don't you let me run you home? There's nothing we can usefully do here.'

'I haven't cashed up for the day,' she said weakly, her thoughts tumbling in confusion.

'Leave it,' Charlie cut in firmly. 'I want you two girls out of here.' He indicated a silent Alan. 'I've a feeling there's going to be some very harsh words spoken around here in a minute.'

'I'll take Jake's car,' Myra said, with an easy assurance which stabbed her heart. But she tried to block her mind to the last time she had climbed into the passenger seat of the low-slung car.

As they sped away, she could see the knot of figures clustering around the damaged aeroplane, whose tail was sticking high in the air. Among them, somewhere, was Jake, no doubt bitterly cursing her for her obstinate selfishness. She looked away before she could pick out his tall, dark figure, and concentrated instead on regaining her composure. He was safe, and that was all that mattered. She mustn't think about him in any other way.

After all, Myra was driving the car in a way that showed she had done it many times before. And on the back seat, next to Jake's briefcase, was a very feminine-looking weekend bag. Myra had come to stay. She was the one who would tonight listen to Jake's account of the afternoon's events. She would soothe him and comfort him and hold him close. While she, Cindy Passmore, would be sitting alone over a boiled egg.

She shook her head in irritation at such weak, self-pitying thoughts. The afternoon's tension had left her sickly shaken. Myra, looking at her passenger's pale face, discreetly lowered the window a little, then began to talk.

'I love this countryside. It's not pretty, like Surrey or Oxfordshire, but it's dramatic and open. It makes you feel free, somehow, as if you've got space, and air to breathe.'

'Yes, it's lovely once you get to know it.'

'How are you finding country life, after London?'

Cindy glanced across in renewed surprise that Myra should know so much about her, and was struck afresh by her dramatic good looks. She was about thirty, and there were fine lines around her eyes which she did not bother to hide. She did not need to. Her dark eyes and glossy hair, her full lips and striking figure, added up to character and beauty.

'I love it. I never did enjoy London much. Too much noise and dirt.'

'You're braver than I am. I couldn't live alone, not in the country. One night without a friendly street light outside my window and I'd be a jibbering wreck.' Myra laughed. 'I'm a real city creature. Although I love to be able to get away whenever I can. Luckily, I've got the opportunity.'

And what an opportunity, Cindy thought bitterly. Jake's country estate was, no doubt, always available to her.

'You turn down here,' she said abruptly, sounding almost sullen.

Myra steered the car to a halt outside Rose Cottage. 'Oh, but it's quite lovely! Jake told me about it, but not how pretty it was!'

She looked up, to the roses rambling around her bedroom window. The bedroom where—she blushed. What else had Jake told Myra? Did they have a *very*

modern relationship? Had he even told her about that
first fateful night when she had first let him stay, then
pushed him away? The colour deepened in her cheeks.
She had wondered whether to ask Myra in for a drink,
but now she realised it was quite impossible. She could
not bear the thought of her seeing the scene of her
devastating humiliation. All she could think of was
hiding herself away.

'Thank you for the lift,' she said hurriedly. 'You can
turn in a gateway, just down the lane.' She opened the
door and got out.

'But your sweater,' Myra said, surprised.

'It doesn't matter. There's no hurry. Thank you for
the lift. I must go.'

Hot-cheeked and awkward with embarrassment, she
stumbled away up her front path.

CHAPTER TEN

THE dark closed in early and the wind blustered menacingly around the cottage, setting her already taut nerves jangling.

She walked restlessly from room to room, unable to settle. Rain splattered against the windows and the fire in the living-room grate refused to draw.

Images tormented her. The dreadful events of the afternoon. Suppose Roddy had been killed? Or, unthinkably, Jake? What if they had crashed on landing, because there was no safe runway to come in on? She must tell Jake as soon as possible that she had changed her mind. He could build as many runways as he wanted.

But when would she see him again? What was he doing now, at this very moment? Were he and Myra curled up together in front of a blazing log fire, Myra perhaps sipping an elegant cocktail, Jake reviving himself with a whisky? Or worse. Perhaps Jake was showering, while Myra brushed out her gorgeous hair in an adjoining bedroom? Perhaps they were going out for a leisurely dinner? Or perhaps they were staying in, having an early night. Perhaps they were already in bed together—

'No. Stop,' she told herself.

Jake was in his elegant manor at one end of the village. She was in her cottage at the other. They were nothing to each other, just boss and employee. She had her own life to live. Her painting. Her friends. She had never minded living alone before, so why, tonight, did she jump at every tap of the roses against the window, every rattle of the front door frame?

She was tired and overwrought, that was why. No matter that it was only eight-thirty. She would have a bath, a light supper, and go to bed.

Half-an-hour later she was in the kitchen, her hair pinned up and damply curling, her feet thrust into mules and her lemon satin dressing gown belted tightly around her. It was an absurd dressing gown for the country, she thought. She should have something warm and woolly, with an old-fashioned tasselled cord. But this remnant of her bridal négligé was still good, not worn or torn, and her budget did not stretch to replacing non-essentials.

More relaxed now, she hummed quietly to herself as she stirred scrambled eggs in a pan. The wind seemed to be dropping a little—or was it?

'Oh!'

There was a sudden howling gust around the cottage. The windows rattled, rain hammered, and in the midst of the noise was a louder, more demanding rat-a-tat-tat on her front door.

'Oh!' she gasped again. Heart hammering, she made her way nervously to the hallway. 'Who is it?'

' 'S me . . . 'S Alan . . .'

'What do you want?'

'Want to come in . . . talk to you . . .'

'What about?'

'Let me in, and I'll tell you.'

His voice sounded slurred and uneven.

'It's getting late. We'll talk tomorrow.'

There was a scuffling noise, then the front door was rattled vigorously. 'Come on, Cindy, open up. We're friends. You said that. Friends . . .' His voice tailed off.

'We *are* friends,' she said firmly. 'But I'm too tired to talk tonight. I'll see you in the club.'

There was a long silence. Had he passed out on her front step? He seemed much the worse for wear. She stepped forward.

'You won't,' said a voice right behind her. 'Been sacked.'

She whirled round.

Alan leaned drunkenly against the kitchen door. Too late, she cursed herself for leaving the back door unlocked after putting the rubbish out.

She stared at him in dismay, and instinctively hugged herself in self-protection as his eyes leered over her scantily clad form.

'Been sacked,' he repeated, and levered himself upright. He began to come towards her.

'Alan, you must go. I want you to leave.'

'Got nowhere to go.'

'Don't be silly. Of course you've got somewhere to go.' She tried to make her voice sound cheerfully practical. 'Look, I'll just put something warmer on, then I'll make you some coffee and you'll feel much better.' She turned to go up the narrow cottage stairs, but he moved quickly to block her path.

'You stay like that,' he ordered. 'That's how I've always imagined you . . . Now I'll find out. Tonight . . .'

He stepped nearer and put his hands round her waist. His alcohol-laden breath forced her to turn her head from him. But she mustn't panic! He had obviously been drinking heavily. She ought to be able to outmanoeuvre him, if she kept her wits about her. Although his grip was surprisingly firm and he seemed steady on his feet.

The grip tightened and he shook her.

'Don't turn away from me like that!' His voice was harsh with hatred. 'You stuck-up little bitch, you always turn away from me. But I'll show you. I'll show you what you've been missing . . .'

'Alan, please!'

'Please, what?' His temper was mounting. His face was an angry red, and his grasp, as he dragged her into the sitting room, was like steel. 'Please, Alan, let's be friends?' He mimicked her cruelly. He flung her down on the sofa and stood over her. 'Little Miss Pretend Virgin, that's you! No wonder your marriage didn't last. Is that what you said to your husband? "No, please"? Well you don't fool me. It's not "No, please" to everyone, is it? Not to Mr High and Mighty himself. He can do what he likes with you, can't he? I've seen it with my own eyes.'

'You're talking nonsense,' she said shakily. 'You don't know what you're saying.'

'No?'

He sat down heavily beside her and leaned over to pin her shoulders back against the sofa. His face was a vicious mask. 'I saw it, remember? That night at the clubhouse after the party. You thought I'd gone, but I was still outside. I saw it all. He took you just like this, didn't he? That bastard.'

Without warning his slack lips lunged for hers.

'Ugh!' With an involuntary cry of disgust she wrenched her head away. Anger and fear gave her the strength to push him violently from her and to jump to her feet.

Alan's lips were twisted in fury, and he got up to come after her.

'If you don't leave me alone, I'll call the police!' Her voice was shrill with panic.

He laughed, horribly. 'Mr Plod on his bike? I'll have got what I want by the time he gets here.'

She backed into a corner as he came towards her.

'Jake Seaton might have taken my job, but he's not going to have everything. I'll get even with him, and you. Tonight I'm going to start with you . . . I'm going to start where he left off . . .'

With unexpected force he suddenly pushed her back against the wall. A hand lashed out and ripped open her gown. 'This is where he got to, isn't it?' he said thickly, and his lips found hers again as a hand came up to knead her breast. Revulsion shuddered through her and she struggled to free herself.

'No, you don't,' he said wetly against her ear. 'You behave with me like you did with him . . . like this . . .'

Violently one of his hands clasped the small of her back close to him, so she felt the full force of his lust for her. She squirmed and fought, but he had her pinned in the corner of the room like a helpless insect. Drunkenness had made him stronger than his slight frame suggested.

'Come on, Cindy, come on,' he urged, breathlessly, as his lips bit at her neck, and his hand roamed her bared breasts. 'You don't want me to hurt you, do you?'

'I want you to go, to leave me alone,' she cried tearfully, but it was useless. Again his revolting lips sought hers. She felt a blackness swimming up, as she suddenly realised he was way past sense or reason.

Yet she must hold on to her own senses, or she was lost! If she could not defeat him by force, then it had to be by guile. Otherwise he would do his worst, and vent all his pent-up anger and resentment on her. She was no longer a person to him. Only a thing, an object. Something to be taken, then flung aside.

The repulsiveness of what her whirling brain now grasped made her go limp with terror. All her limbs were like jelly.

But Alan, confusedly sensing a change in her, drew back his head and looked blearily at her. 'You see,' he muttered in slurry tones, 'you want it too. I knew you did. We don't have to fight.' His embrace slackened slightly, and she took the opportunity to edge away from him. Her heart was pounding, but her mind was clear. Almost casually she shifted within his arms and was able to pull the edges of her robe together.

'No, it's silly, all this fighting.' She swallowed. 'You can stay here tonight—with me. We can take our time. We don't have to hurry things.'

Averting her gaze from the throb of a vein at his temple, his wet fish eyes, she gave him a playful push, which allowed her just enough room to step out of her imprisoning corner. From the corner of her eye she caught sight of the clock on the mantleshelf. Unbelievably, it was still only quarter past nine. Centuries had passed in the last few minutes!

'Come and sit down,' she coaxed, taking his hand and pulling him to the sofa. Her gorge rose when her flesh met his again but she fought to conceal it— everything depended on managing to contain his anger.

Alan slumped against the cushions, a triumphant

smile on his face. He tried to pull her down with him, but she playfully resisted.

'Hey, what's all the hurry? I've given in, haven't I?' She tried to laugh. 'But you must have had a dreadful day. Let me get you something to eat, or coffee. Or a drink if you want it—there's some whisky, I think.' His eyes narrowed suspiciously. Her tone was unconvincing, and even his befuddled senses knew it.

'I don't want any more of your games. I've wasted enough time. You know what I've come for.'

Her heart began to knock with fear again.

'Yes.' Her throat was dry. 'Well, look . . . Give me a few minutes, Alan. Let me go to the bathroom. I'll give you a call when I'm ready. The bedroom's on the left, at the top of the stairs.'

He obviously still didn't trust her, but he did not try to stop her leaving.

In the bathroom, the door locked, she began to quake and tremble. But she forced herself to keep control. With a bit of luck Alan might fall asleep, which would give her some chance of escape. But she obviously couldn't count on it. It was impossible to know just how much he had drunk, or what state of mind he was in. Certainly he was angry enough to be completely ruthless; bitter enough to exact any punishment. He was dangerous to her.

Swiftly she searched the room for some useful weapon of self-defence, but there was nothing. Only a long-handled plastic lavatory brush, and somehow that did not seem designed for violent conflict.

'Cindy, where are you?' His voice came from the bottom of the stairs.

'Just a minute. I'll only be a minute.'

She thought quickly. Her bedroom had a key . . . it might just work.

Silently she opened the bathroom door and tiptoed across the narrow landing. It was hard to ease the key from the inside of the bedroom door without making a noise but somehow she managed it. But there was no time to push it back into the outside of the lock, as she had planned, because Alan's tread was on the stair.

Swiftly she fled back into the darkened bathroom. Everything hinged on what he did now. If he turned into the bedroom, it might be all right. But if he came searching for her in the bathroom . . .

His tread was within a couple of feet of her. He hesitated, then pushed open her bedroom door.

'Cindy? Cindy, put the light on. I can't see a damned thing.' She hesitated, willing him to go on further into the room.

He did so, stumbling against the bed.

At that moment she sprang forward, pulling the door closed and fumbling to insert the key in the lock. Her nervous fingers dropped it. 'Damn!'

'You little trickster!'

With all her strength she hung on to the doorknob and searched frantically for the key. Her fingers closed on it just as Alan began to wrench at the door. The key slid into the lock.

'You bitch! You've really done it now! I won't forget this!'

She turned it. She was safe. For the moment.

The door rattled, but the lock seemed solid.

What now, though? She could not flee the cottage on a night like this in just a dressing gown, and her clothes were locked in with Alan. Perhaps she should just stick it out till the morning? Sober, he would surely come to his senses?

A crashing sweep from inside the room told her otherwise. In anger, he had obviously lain waste to the things on her dressing table.

Running downstairs she phoned Betty and Geoff. There was no reply. She tried the only other number she knew by heart. The flying club.

'Yes?' Jake's voice was curt.

'Oh!' The sound of his voice took her totally aback. She had not really dared hope anyone would still be there. Let alone—— Suddenly she began to sob wildly with relief.

'It's me. Cindy. I'm so sorry. But you see——'

'Cindy. What is it?' His voice sounded sharp. With an enormous effort she pulled herself together.

'It's Alan,' she stammered out. 'He's drunk and—and a bit violent. He just turned up here out of the blue. I don't know what to do.'

'Has he,' Jake paused, 'harmed you?'

'No—but I think he might.'

There was an audible intake of breath.

'Where is he now?'

'In the bedroom.'

'I'll come over.'

'I didn't mean to bother you——' But the phone had already been slammed down.

She slumped on the sofa, a confused heap of emotions. There was the enormous relief of knowing help was at hand—help in the form of masterful, steadfast Jake. But Jake had sounded curt and angry. Now she would have two difficult men to deal with— and the last thing she wanted was to be beholden to Jake in any way.

No doubt he was cursing her as he drove down the lane. Whatever had been keeping him at the clubhouse, he was bound to want to hurry home to Myra. Weak and weary, she buried her head in her hands.

About two minutes later the car drew up and Jake ran to the front door. He took in her satin-clad appearance with one penetrating, contemptuous glance.

'Where is he now?'

'In the bedroom still—I locked him in.'

For the briefest moment his mouth quirked in humour. Then he was quizzing her.

'What sort of state is he in?'

'I don't really know. He must have had quite a lot to drink to be so—so forceful.'

Jake shot her a dark look. 'I heard him smash something in my room. But I think he's sober enough to know what he's doing.' Tears of weariness and shock pricked behind her eyes. 'He frightened me.'

Jake's face took on a granite anger. He looked so massive and resolute in her tiny hallway that she felt a qualm. What if her own tiredness and tension had exaggerated the situation? 'But he was upset about losing his job and everything,' she added lamely.

'He should have thought about that before,' said Jake, going up the stairs.

From below she heard the key turn, then two voices, one sullen, one stern. As the two men came back down the stairs she turned away and went into the kitchen, sickened by the whole episode. No one spoke to her and within seconds she heard the car draw away. It was very quiet in the cottage. She leaned wearily against the table, not thinking or moving. Then, walking like an invalid, she laboriously climbed the stairs and surveyed the mess in her bedroom.

As she had surmised, her bottles and jars had been swept to the floor and a pot of cleansing cream was seeping on to the carpet. Her bed looked rumpled and used—Alan must have flung back the covers in his restless anger.

She shuddered at the sight, then jumped as the front door knocker sounded.

'It's all right. It's me,' Jake said.

She ran down.

'I took him to the village and left him by the telphone box,' Jake said, coming in. 'He can either walk home or get a taxi. I don't much care which. Can I wash my hands? I had to stop and push him into a hedge to be sick, on the way.'

'Of course, the bathroom's upstairs.'

But he would know that. She blushed.

She stood waiting for him in the living room.

'I can't thank you enough——' she began, but Jake's face was set and cold, and her words faded out.

'Have you seen the mess in your bedroom?' he asked. 'Things all over the place and the bed well rumpled—or was it like that before things turned nasty?'

She looked at him in horror. Her face went white as

it dawned on her exactly how the scene must appear to him.

There she was in her dressing gown. The bed was rumpled. A man violent with frustration had to be evicted . . .

'It isn't how you think!' she burst out. 'I was going to bed. I was tired, and unhappy. He just burst in through the back door.'

'But you *had* been seeing him.' It was a statement, not a question.

'Only as friends. That was the trouble. That was why he wanted to get his own back.'

'That's understandable,' Jake said coldly.

Colour flushed to her cheeks.

'You seem to make something of a habit of this kind of scene. Perhaps you enjoy them?' Ironic scorn tinged his voice.

'That's not fair!'

'Isn't it? Well then, Cindy Passmore, I can only conclude that you have a very poor understanding of the average human male. "Only as friends" wouldn't be good enough for young Jenkins for very long. Anyone could have told you that. He's far too much the young buck, out to prove himself, to stand for that kind of arrangement. As for your behaviour in other direc-tions——' He bit off his words and turned away from her. His eye fell on the sullen fire, which he abruptly bent down to, to stir vigorously to life. She could not stand it. His contempt and his scorn of her. Something inside her snapped and she was suddenly shouting at the top of her lungs.

'All right, I made a mistake! I didn't know what Alan was really like! I was lonely, and he seemed good company. Is it such a crime to go on picnics with someone, or to the cinema, without wanting to hop into bed with them? If it is then I'm glad I'm a criminal! As for tonight—well I know what you're thinking, but it wasn't like that. He burst in on me after I'd had a bath. That's why I'm dressed like this. And the bed's only rumpled because he must have done it ... Perhaps he even heard me on the phone to you ... He might have wanted you to think ... Oh, I don't know what!'

'That the two of you had been in just the position that the two of us were once in!' Jake concluded for her. Anger was in his face as he straightened up from the fire. 'That he had very good reason for his frustration! That the girl in his arms had been promising him the universe—until she got cold feet!'

He strode towards her and stood close up to her. 'If that was the case, I understand his feelings all too well!' His eyes—cold, dark, penetrating—locked with hers. A tremor of tension passed between them. Suddenly she was hugging herself, warding off shivers which threatened to wrack her slight frame.

'It wasn't,' she said through gritted teeth. 'It *wasn't*. How many times do I have to tell you? I wish you'd never got involved in all this. I only phoned the club because it was a number I could remember.'

'That's a fine way to say thank you,' he ground out. 'Well I, too, wish I'd never got involved. Don't you think I've had enough for one day? Without having to sort out the sordid little private lives of my employees? I'm a pilot not a personnel officer, and I don't mind telling you that I'd far rather be at home soaking in a hot bath than running drunks out of people's houses.'

For the first time she took in his appearance. He was still dressed for London, in his smart dark suit, although somewhere along the line his tie had been discarded and his shirt was open low enough to show the shadowing of dark hair on his broad chest. He looked tired, and through her anger came an overwhelming longing to hold out her arms and draw him close. But he had Myra to do that for him, lovely Myra who was no doubt at that moment listening for his car to sweep up the gravelled drive home.

The thought of Myra rekindled her bitterness.

'Well, I'm not stopping you,' she snapped out. 'I am grateful for what you've done, believe me, but I don't think that means I've got to listen to lots of unfair accusations afterwards. *I've* had enough for today, as well!'

'Have you?' he queried. Their glances, full of pent-up antagonism, locked in mutual hostility. Tension pulsed between them, rising like a tide. He took another step closer and she could see the rapid rise and fall of his chest as he struggled to contain his emotions. 'Not quite, I think. Perhaps you should show me exactly how grateful you are?'

Then his arms were reaching out and drawing her purposefully to him, and his lips were finding hers with a peremptory passion. She struggled in his embrace, twisting her head in an attempt to evade his lips, fighting backwards in his arms.

But, unlike Alan, he was one hundred per cent sober, and ruthlessly determined. As she fought, he tightened his hold of her. His hands moulded the curves of her back through the thin stuff of her gown. One reached up to tangle in her hair and to hold her lips to his. Her shudders of anger began to change to a different kind of tremor. She struggled. She had to. But it was useless.

Using all his skill and experience, Jake broke through her defences. He was not gentle or loving, but cold and determined. His lips explored hers with a certainty of ownership, parting her mouth so he could claim her further. His hands brought her closer, knowing the curves of her shoulders and waist, pressing her close to him, so she would know how much he wanted her.

'No, Jake, no!' She twisted her mouth from him and cried out against his shoulder, but her body betrayed her. As if with a mind of its own, it clung to his, trembling from his touch. For the briefest moment he looked at her, at her averted head. His eyes took in her cheek against his suit, the line of her bare shoulder, and his hands released her slightly so that she was held in an almost gentle embrace which made her quiver with desire for him. Yet summoning all her mental strength, she managed to make herself try and break from his hold. In response his hands moved to take her head between them. Then his lips found hers again and his tongue plundered her mouth until she was weak, and all rebellion had left her. His hands moved down her neck and throat, sending white fire through her veins. They parted her robe and held each small, full breast. When he bent to kiss their taut tips, she made no protest. Not then, nor when his hands loosened the tie of her robe and explored each curve and hollow beneath. She could not speak, nor move. Her whole being—mind, spirit and body—was afire with love and need for him.

Masterfully he pushed her back among the same cushions where Alan had lolled earlier. Her gown was parted and she did not care. All that mattered was Jake, letting him see how much she loved him. He kissed her again, and his hands laid claim to her. This was the moment. He would take her, and it was all in the world she wanted. Let thought come tomorrow. Flushed, dishevelled, her lips reddened from his rough kisses, she reached up her arms to draw him closer still.

But he was levering himself upright, breaking her hold as easily and carelessly as a lion might snap through cotton.

'I think enough is enough, don't you?' he said grimly, and his eyes flicked contemptuously over her half-naked and abandoned form. '*This* time *I'll* be the one who gets to say "when".'

'Oh!' Dismay caught at her throat, as her hands clutched convulsively at the open folds of her gown.

Jake got up and stood looking down at her.

'A taste of your own medicine. Isn't that what it's called? Perhaps, now, Cindy Passmore, you might have a little more respect for people's feelings. Or are you still as selfish as ever?'

With a lithe step he walked out, no backward glance impeding his departure. She heard the front door close, his step on the path, the garden gate, the car engine.

Then there was silence, broken only by the lonely hooting of an owl.

With a huge, shuddering sigh she began to sob and shake as if she would never, ever stop.

CHAPTER ELEVEN

THE days passed in a blur. She told Charlie she was ill, and could not get to work, and it was almost true. Her limbs felt heavy, her head was thick, and it was an effort to crawl out of bed. She tried to block from her memory that evening's ghastly events yet, perversely, Jake still invaded her every thought.

If only she could see him again—explain—make him understand. But his mind was made up about her. She was a selfish, stupid girl who deserved nothing but unhidden contempt.

On Thursday, when she was sitting desolately at the kichen table, too weary to move, Betty knocked on the back door.

'Early closing,' she said, taking off her coat, 'so I thought I'd pop down and see you. I wanted to ask you about Saturday, what you're going to do.'

'Saturday?' Cindy said, feeling dull-witted.

'Yes, Saturday. The club dinner and dance. I mean, you were going with Alan, weren't you? But I don't suppose he'll want to put in an appearance now he's been fired.'

'Oh. No. I don't suppose he will.'

'Cindy, love, are you all right? You look pale.' Betty scrutinised her. 'Shall I make us a cup of tea? And it's a bit chilly in here. Shall I light the oven to warm the place up? You know, there was a really harsh frost last night—the lane's still slippery in places. Mind you, we're only a few weeks off Christmas, so I suppose we've got to expect it.'

Somehow Betty's cheerful chatter managed to break her gloom enough for her to smile and put on some pretence of normality.

'I've had a few days off work,' she said as they sat

down with their steaming cups. 'I think I must have caught a chill, or something. I just didn't feel up to anything.' That last sentence, at least, was true.

Betty clucked and fussed, advising hot drinks and a good rest.

'What do you think about Saturday, then,' she said as she got up to go. 'Will you be well enough to go, do you think, or not? Only Geoff and I were wondering whether you'd like to join our party? Some of Geoff's old friends are coming up from London, and his sister and her husband will be there.'

'I haven't got a partner,' Cindy said. 'You're right about Alan. The last thing he would want to do, I should think, is to go to the Christmas dinner and dance. Not that I'm in touch with him,' she added hastily. 'For all I know he might have left the area.'

'That's no problem. There'll be several spare men in the group. We can all swop around for dances. It'll be fun. Do come—if you feel well enough, of course.'

'I'd like to,' she said slowly. Not because it would be fun. The way she felt, there would never be any fun, ever again. But because Jake would be there, and every cell in her body hungered to see him again.

Of course, it would be across a crowded room, and he would be there with Myra, and there would be no chance to speak to him. But just to see him! Those dark eyes. That commanding form ... 'Yes, I'd like to. Thank you very much for asking me.'

Betty looked at her oddly. 'Are you sure you're all right, Cindy? You don't seem quite yourself. I worry about you—whether you're eating enough and looking after yourself properly.'

'Of course I am, Betty. Don't be silly.' She stood up, changing the subject. 'What's it like, the dinner and dance? Is it very grand? What should I wear?'

Betty assured her that in spite of the black tie invitation, the accent was on fun rather than formality and they spent a comfortable few minutes discussing clothes and other easy topics.

Betty's visit injected her with enough energy to do some more work on her painting of the Pitts Special, Jake's aeroplane. She sensed it was good, and the feeling excited her, combining with the tremulous anticipation of seeing Jake again to make her feel keyed up and restless.

So much so that, by Saturday night, her nerves were as stretched as fine tuning wires. She walked up the lane early, and changed into her sea green watered silk evening dress at Betty and Geoff's. Betty gasped in open appreciation as she twirled in front of the mirror. 'You'll be the hit of the evening, Cindy. Look at the way it sets off the colour of your hair! No one will be able to hold a candle to you.'

'It's the only evening dress I've ever owned,' she confessed. 'I've had it ever since I was at college. A friend who was doing dress design made it for me. It's absolutely ancient now, but I've always loved it.' It was true that the shoestring straps flattered her slim shoulders and the floating hem made her seem as fragile as china, but she was paler than usual and her eyes looked large and haunted as she cast one backward glance in the mirror. A dusting of heightened colour along her cheekbones hinted at the suppressed excitement she felt, but luckily no one could know how sick with nerves she was, as longing and dread mingled in her stomach in equal measure.

Betty and Geoff's group was big and boisterous enough to accept her into its midst without any effort on her part. She smiled at the jokes, knowing enough flying jargon by now to understand the more technical ones, and sipped cautiously at her drink—in her state, she knew, it would be all too easy to fall back on Dutch courage.

By the time they arrived at the grand country manor hotel where the dance was taking place it was already quite late and her stomach knotted with anticipation as they walked into the room. But Jake was not there. A large table at the top of the room stood empty among the crowds of familiar faces—engineers and air traffic controllers and student pilots. She greeted them smilingly, but her smile was tight with disappointment. Jake would not come now. The waitresses were already serving the soup.

But for Betty's sake she must try and make an effort, she told herself, and listened politely as Geoff's brother-in-law told her about his motor spares business in Manchester. He had complicated problems with his distribution network, and was outlining these at length when she raised her head and found herself looking directly at Jake.

Her heart turned over. He was looking straight at her as he passed her table, a dark enigmatic glance. In his black dinner jacket and white silk shirt he looked devastating. She could hardly breathe. Then he looked away and the moment was past.

She watched him thread his way towards the top table. Ahead of him was Myra, stunning in a silver shimmering sheath of expensive fashion. Behind them were others of their group, groomed and expensive looking. A buzz of excitement went round the room. Geoff said, 'My goodness, all the big boys are here tonight.' He pointed out champion flyers from America and Germany, a Dutch racing driver and a Canadian skiing ace. With them were glamorous girls, whose presence quite outshone the healthy country good looks of the other women in the room. Betty nudged her and said, 'Look, next to Myra Collingdale. Isn't that Jeanette whatsit, who's in that new musical . . .?'

She could not reply. All the tension, the anticipation, the faint, lingering hope had seeped away from her. Jake was here now. But it was Jake in his own world—a glamorous, exciting, sophisticated, international world. For the first time, it seemed, she was seeing him as he really was. Someone quite beyond her reach. A man at the top of his tree, with the world at his feet.

She could hardly bear to look, and yet she could not look away. With awful fascination she watched him help Myra into her seat. She saw him smile and attend to a willowy blonde girl—a Swedish photographic model, someone said—who was sitting opposite him. Whatever he said made the girl smile beautifully at him. He leant back, his arm extended casually along Myra's chairback. He shared a joke with two of the men, then beckoned the waitress to bring their belated food. She watched him reach for his glass and set it back down. Her own food was forgotten. Then he looked up, and his glance was directly for her. The shock made her tremble and look quickly away.

She should not have come. She realised that now. It was making everything far worse. She felt as if her heart was breaking inside, and the rest of the meal passed in slow agony as she schooled herself to keep from looking in the only direction her eyes wanted to go.

When the band began to play she was able to occupy herself dancing with first one, then another in the party. Charlie Yeats came over and steered her around the floor in a stately waltz, and then several of the club's pupils asked her to dance. Under any other circumstances she would have been having a splendid time, enjoying herself among friends. But she was sick with pent-up misery and her smile was kept in place by will-power alone.

The music stopped. Her partner released her and began to walk her back to her table. As they walked the music started up again, slow and mellow. And then Jake was beside her, taking her smoothly into his arms and leading her back among the dancers.

She said nothing. She was speechless.

After a time he said conversationally. 'You seem about as cheerful as a wet weekend.'

'I'm sorry.'

'Don't you like dancing?'

'Yes. But not tonight.'

It was taking every ounce of her concentration not to tremble in his embrace. His nearness made her head spin with longing. In desperation she fixed her mind on his contemptuous words to her, the last time she had seen him.

'Is it the occasion—or is it me? You didn't look exactly ecstatic earlier, I grant you. But you looked a damn sight happier than you do now.'

'I just haven't been feeling too good this week.'

'That makes two of us.'

'Oh!' Surprise made her glance up, her eyes locking with his. Then she remembered. 'I suppose it was awful for you—thinking one of your pupils might have been lost.' His eyes had been shadowed with fatigue when he arrived at Rose Cottage that evening.

'I've recovered from that,' he said, 'although it was no thanks to you.'

His words made her stop abruptly, the low music forgotten. Among the swaying couples they were the only point of stillness, but neither of them noticed.

'What do you mean?'

'It shouldn't have happened,' he rapped out. 'It shouldn't have been as bad as it was. If we had had that second runway at least the only problem would have been steering the lad home. As it was, he did well to put the aircraft down in one piece under those conditions.'

His eyes were hard and without mercy. His hands still held her, but in challenge only.

She took a deep, shaky breath and met his eyes, her chin up. 'You're right. You must have that runway. I won't stop you building it. It's something I've been thinking about ever since I started work at the club. I'd virtually made up my mind before what happened this week, although I don't suppose you'll believe that.'

His eyes scoured her face, upturned to his. There was a long moment of tension. Then his mouth curved into a deep, warm smile. His hands on her shoulders shifted slightly, as if to hold her with warmth, not hatred.

'If you really mean that, then I can't thank you enough. It means more than I can tell you.'

Her eyes sparked. 'What do you mean—"if I really mean that"? Don't you believe me?'

His mouth quirked. 'I know you can change your mind.'

'Oh!' Colour flushed into her face. Was he never going to let her forget? With a gasp she broke away from him and ran blindly off the dance floor. Breaking through the heavy swing doors she found herself in a quiet, carpeted corridor. She hesitated, then ran the way that seemed to promise fresh air and freedom. But the corridor ended in a cul-de-sac of locked doors.

'Cindy.' Jake had followed her. Now he stood blocking her path as she ran back. He grasped her elbows firmly as she tried to get past him.

'Calm down,' he said. 'I didn't mean to upset you like that. I was simply telling the truth. It's a bad habit of mine.'

'Let me go,' she said through gritted teeth. 'Haven't you got what you want from me? Why do you have to torment me further?' She stared at the ground, not at him, and stood rigid and still in his grasp. To her surprise he dropped his hands.

Summoning all her reserves she looked at him steadily, the strength of character she had acquired at such cost in London now coming to her aid.

'Yes,' she said shakily, 'I *did* change my mind that night. I got carried away—but not quite enough to forget what you really wanted from me. Not enough to forget about the runway. But did I commit such a terrible crime? And if so, haven't you punished me enough? You seem to want to remind me of my sin in rejecting you at every turn!'

'Surely you didn't think——' he began, but she went on, determined to say her piece.

'As for the runway—you thought it was selfishness that made me refuse your request, well maybe it was. But not in the way you think. It was to honour the wishes of an old woman. Aunt Beth entrusted Rose Cottage to me in her will to keep in peace and tranquillity. "As I would have wanted it." Those were her very words. And the last thing she would have wanted was her wishes about the runway counteracted at the first opportunity.'

'So why have you now changed your mind?' Jake's voice was low, quiet.

She hesitated, searching for the right words. 'Because life is more important than death,' she said finally. 'The safety of people alive now is more important than the wishes of a dead woman. I know that now. Aunt Beth wasn't in her right mind towards the end. She wouldn't really have wanted to put people's lives at risk. And she did want me to have peace of mind—I can only have that if I do what I think is right.'

She lowered her head to the carpet, unable to bear Jake's intent gaze. They stood silent, a foot apart. The only sound was from the distant ballroom, where the band had struck up a lively foxtrot. Suddenly she felt completely exhausted.

'Cindy——' Jake began, and took her elbow.

At that moment the doors burst open and Myra shimmered out in silver. 'Jake, you'll be needed in a minute,' she called. 'They want you to present the cups.'

Cindy snatched her arm away, terrified of what Myra might think of the scene. But Myra stopped abruptly as she saw the two of them together and said simply, 'Oh, I'm sorry.'

Cindy met the other woman's glance and a curious understanding seemed to well up between them. 'Excuse me,' she said, flustered, and took the opportunity to slip out past Jake and away.

Back in the ballroom she snatched her evening bag from the table, whispering to Betty that she felt unwell and was leaving early.

'How will you get home?' Betty said, worriedly starting up.

'There are taxis waiting outside. I saw them earlier,' she whispered, pushing Betty back down into her seat. 'Please let me slip away quietly,' she pleaded urgently. 'I don't want anyone to make a fuss. I'm sorry to spoil your party.' She turned and fled before Betty could protest, out of the ballroom, down to the front entrance and out into the chill December air. Running in her long dress as if to put a million miles between herself and Jake Seaton.

But as she stepped into the first taxi waiting on the frosty gravel, he came quickly out of the front entrance.

'Cindy——'

She turned to shut the car door, but he moved quickly forward and held it open.

'Cindy, what the hell are you doing?'

'Leave me alone, Jake. You've got what you wanted now.'

He muttered a rough curse. 'Is that what you think? Well if you refuse to talk to me now, I'll see you at the club tomorrow.'

'I don't think so. I'm leaving the job.' There was no question about it. Working with Jake was no longer bearable. She longed for him, but he despised her, and seemed determined to remind her of it at every turn.

'Leaving? Why? What's got into you?'

'I would have thought it was perfectly obvious,' she said bitterly. A child of three could see her love for him, she was sure.

He dashed back his cuff to look impatiently at his watch, knowing he was needed for the ceremonies inside, and she used the moment to pull the car door from him.

'Cindy, *please*!' His tone was one of utter exasperation.

'Leave me alone, Jake Seaton. I've had enough. I've said it before, and I'll say it again—I don't want to see you again. Ever.'

CHAPTER TWELVE

SHE was ill, she had to be. Why else did her head ache so badly, and her limbs feel too heavy to lift out of bed each morning? All the sick weariness she had felt before the night of the dinner and dance now returned, a hundred times worse.

Since that dreadful evening she had only made one positive act—telephoning Charlie Yeats to tender her resignation. It felt bad to leave him in the lurch like that, but with winter closing in early this year there were fewer students than usual, and she knew the club would manage without her.

That had been four, or was it five days ago?

The days and nights seemed to be blurring into each other. Betty had called round on the morning after the dinner, but she had convinced her that her malaise was a simple case of lingering 'flu, and that what she needed most was rest and quiet.

Since then the silence of the cottage had closed around her. She had tried to paint, but instead spent hours just staring at the canvas, not seeing her work but only Jake, his gypsy wildness and dark contemptuous eyes. He was an impossible man, arrogant and impatient. Yet she loved him and wanted him—and could never have him. Wandering aimlessly from room to room she could see him standing as he had once stood at her living-room window, or leaning self-confidently in her bedroom doorway.

It was frightening how little control she had over her thoughts. Jake filled her mind. Her rigorous self-control, built up so painstakingly over the years, was now crumbling to nothing, and as it did so the past flooded back to haunt her.

She loved Jake, she acknowledged to herself, in a way

she had never loved her husband. Perhaps she had never loved Simon at all? Which made everything that had happened infinitely worse. The nightmares came back, and she would wake sweating and shaking to the darkness of the isolated cottage, her mind reliving again that last, terrible evening.

Then, too, she had lost control. Simon had come home late, later than ever. The supper she had so lovingly prepared was a burnt cinder, and she had taken up her habitual station by the plate glass window, staring out at the world beyond her marriage.

'Mooning over the view again,' Simon had said aggressively, as he wrinkled his nose over the charred food, and her control had begun to slip.

'Does it matter to you *what* I do, just as long as I'm waiting here for you when you get home?' Her voice had been sharp.

'Well, I think you might find something a bit more constructive to do than that. You could learn to cook, for a start.'

'I *can* cook—but I can't work miracles. I can't make things taste just as good as three hours after they were ready!'

'Oh, time-keeping now, are you? You want to be careful, Cindy, you're turning into a typical bored housewife!'

'*You* wanted me to be a housewife! *You* wanted me to be at home all day! It was *you* who said I couldn't finish my studies!'

'And now you're fostering a grudge against me.' He had leant back in his chair, tipping up the legs, and said coldly, 'You know, if you go on like this you'll be a proper shrew before you're thirty.'

She had turned white-faced back to the window, hiding the tears that his cruel remark had prompted. The awful thing was that there was truth in his observation. Bitterness seemed to be growing inside her like a poisonous weed. But her turned back had prompted Simon to sudden, violent rage.

'Cindy. You look at me!' he had shouted. She had not turned round. 'I suppose you regret marrying me!' he had shouted, then, to her obstinate back.

'Yes,' she had sobbed. 'Yes, I do.'

There had been a long, fearful silence. Then Simon had come up behind her and said viciously into her ear. 'Good. Then that makes two of us! At least we agree on something!' And he had picked up his coat and slammed out.

Out to where and what she had never known. It must have been about ten at night when he left, although she had never been able to be precise when the police had questioned her later. The crash had happened in the early hours of the next morning. They said he must have drunk a bottle of whisky, at least. Had he been drinking earlier that evening, the police had wanted to know? She had not been able to tell them. Why would he be driving west out of London? She had no idea. She had been a terrible wife, it was plain, knowing and caring nothing about her husband's movements. And finally she had driven him to his death. No one ever said it, but it was what they were all thinking. And *she* knew it was true.

Now that knowledge, pushed down hard for so many years, had sprung back to haunt her. Jake had called her selfish, and he was absolutely right. Her selfish admission had driven Simon from home. More recently, her selfishness had hurt Jake's pride, and Alan's, too. Even her loyal friend Betty had been touched by it. Hadn't she fled in panic from the dinner and dance, casting a blight on the evening for everyone in Betty's party? And that simply because she had wanted to get away?

She was fit for nothing but a hermit's existence ... maybe she would become old and slightly mad, like poor Aunt Beth ... the roses would grow across the front path, and the doors would sag on their hinges ... Rose Cottage would shelter her, but would never be the peaceful haven her aunt had wished for her ...

One day when she got out of bed her legs buckled beneath her. Picking herself up shakily from the rug, she realised she had eaten nothing for days but a few biscuits. Shocked, she forced herself to drink some coffee and to eat some breakfast cereal. The food tasted like sawdust and seemed to stick in her throat.

As she ate, the telephone rang. She eyed it warily, hoping it would stop, but when the ringing persisted she knew she would have to make the effort to answer it.

'Hello?'

'It's Sarah. Cindy, where have you *been*? I've been ringing you for days.'

'Oh.'

Sometimes she had dozed fitfully in the day, but she had thought the telephone she heard was in her dreams. 'Um. I've had a touch of 'flu.'

'Are you sure that's all? You sound a bit odd.'

'No, really, I'm fine.'

'What are you doing at Christmas? I'm ringing to see if you'd like to come down to Paul's parents with us? I don't like to think of you out in the wilds all alone.'

'Christmas,' she said cautiously. Her mind really wasn't working normally. She knew it was some time soon, but when? Whatever she said, she mustn't let Sarah see how far her grasp on reality had slipped.

'Yes, Christmas,' Sarah said patiently. 'This weekend. Friday's Christmas Eve. You must have thought about your plans.'

'Oh, yes.' She laughed, a slightly high-pitched laugh. 'Sorry, I'm feeling a bit cotton woolly. I expect it's the 'flu. Er, there's quite a lot going on here, actually. What with Betty and Geoff and the club and everything . . .' Her voice tailed off. She looked out of the window for inspiration. Sarah was not easily deceived. The scene was bleak and grey-looking. A robin huddled for warmth among the bare rose stems. 'Anyway the weather looks really awful. I wouldn't want to leave the cottage if the pipes were likely to freeze up, or there was snow forecast. Thanks awfully, Sarah, I do appreciate it. But I really think I'd better stay put.'

'Well, that's a shame. We would have loved to have you. How much holiday have you got? Could you join us later?'

'Holiday?'

'From the club.'

'Oh, I've—er—got as much time as I like.'

'Cindy,' Sarah said suspiciously, 'you sound most peculiar——'

'I'm perfectly all right,' she cut in, an edge of near-panic in her voice. 'I really am. Sarah, I'll have to go—there's something boiling in the kitchen.' She put the phone down with a bang, her heart racing. Contact with another human being, even a perfectly friendly one like Sarah, imposed an impossible strain on her. She swallowed.

Was she really all right? Or not? What was happening to her?

Whatever it was, it frightened her.

CHAPTER THIRTEEN

THE robin on the kitchen windowsill looked cold and hungry. Frost had crusted the garden with white, and the sky threatened snow. Those sunny autumn mornings when she had first worked at the flying club seemed worlds away from this bleak Christmas Eve.

Crumbling a handful of bread she stepped out into the garden. Everything was quiet. Even her footsteps sounded muffled by the cold. Everything, that is, except one clear noise . . . the buzz of an engine . . . near at hand . . . She looked up. Quite close, above the airfield, the Pitts was being put through its paces, wheeling and diving in elaborate manoeuvres. Even on a winter's day like this, it seemed, Jake was pushing himself hard, seeking perfection. She stood, bread forgotten in her hand, watching the aeroplane spin and turn, remote and out of reach. Jake would be thinking only of his flying. Never had she felt quite so desolate, so lonely and bereft, as standing in this wintry garden, watching a dancing speck against the heavy grey clouds.

'Cindy!'

She whipped round. Jake stood at the corner of the cottage.

'You?' She looked in bewilderment from his dark figure to the aeroplane.

'Mike Peel,' he said briefly. 'An American friend of mine. He wanted to try out my machine.'

She stood stunned. He walked forward.

'Cindy, what in God's name do you think you're doing?' He stepped still nearer, an angry look on his face. She shrank back from him, looking down as he gesticulated.

'I——'

'Look at you! Out here in this weather in just a

174

nightdress!' As if to reinforce his words, a first few fine snowflakes drifted down between them.

'I only came out for a moment, to feed the robin.' Surprise and shock made her instinctively defensive.

Jake took her arm and looked her up and down, his eyes dark. 'What on earth have you been doing to yourself? You're as thin as a rake.' It was true. Her wrists were as slender as sparrow bones. 'You'd better get inside and put some warm clothes on.'

Without pausing to hear her protests, he hustled her into the kitchen.

'Now go upstairs and get dressed, while I make you some hot coffee.'

She stood rooted to the spot, staring at him with wide eyes. She had thought about him so much that the real man, standing next to her, was almost too powerful to cope with. In his flying boots and jacket, over jeans and a thick cream sweater, he seemed massively strong and forbidding.

'Are you going—or do I have to take you up there and do it for you?'

'I——' Her throat was too dry for speech.

'And while you're doing that, pack some things.'

'Pack—what for?' Finally she had managed to croak out a sentence.

'I know you said you never wanted to see me again,' he said grimly, 'but I'm not leaving you here alone at Christmas. Not in this state. You're coming back with me.'

She looked at him with huge, puzzled eyes.

'Your friend Sarah was worried about you,' he said in explanation. 'She phoned the flying club. And now I see the state you're in, I can see she had every reason to be worried.'

'Sarah spoke to you?' she stammered out.

'No, to Charlie. He got straight on to me. Old Charlie sees more than he says,' he added, enigmatically.

'I'm all right,' she protested. 'I really am.' She seemed to have been saying nothing else to people for days.

'Nonsense. You're as pale as a ghost and half-starved.' He put out a hand towards her, almost as if he would ease back a lock of hair from her face, then dropped it abruptly and turned to fill the kettle. 'You look as if you haven't slept in weeks, either.'

'I don't want to go home with you!' It would be torture to spend Christmas with Jake, and no doubt Myra, too. Especially as a semi-invalid, someone they were forced to be kind to.

'I'm not giving you any choice. Even if I have to put you under my arm and carry you there.'

She swallowed.

'You've got three minutes to go and get dressed. After that, I come and help you.'

Stunned by the unexpected turn of events, and browbeaten by Jake's curt commands she went mechanically upstairs and put on jeans and a sweater. No wonder he seemed so angry. The last thing he would want was his Christmas blighted by her tiresome troubles.

'Where's your case?' he asked, as she came back downstairs. She regarded him with silent mutiny.

'All right then——' He got up from his chair and headed towards the stairs.

'No! I'll get it!' There would be no deflecting him. Somehow she would have to endure the next few days. The festive season, she thought ironically, and felt perilously near to tears.

'Cindy,' he called from the bottom of the stairs, 'pack that dress you were wearing at the dinner and dance the other night. I've some friends staying for Christmas, and there may well be some celebrating to do.'

Dully she did as she was told. Torture was being added to torture. Whatever celebrating Jake's friends would be doing, would mean nothing to her.

He locked the cottage carefully behind them and ushered her into his car. On the journey they were both silent. Jake's mood seemed blacker still, and she had no resources or energy to draw on.

The silence between them meant she could take in his house without distraction. Close to it was everything she had imagined. Even on this chill day it looked mellow and peaceful. There was an old-fashioned holly wreath on the white front door and the huge brass knocker gleamed with fresh polishing. They swept up the drive and Jake skidded to a halt by the shallow entrance steps. There was a log fire burning in the stone fireplace in the hall, and another, cosier fire in the airy drawing room he led her into.

'Sit down,' he said, guiding her into one corner of a huge chintz settee that was drawn up to the flames. She did as he told her and felt the heat of the fire begin to penetrate through to her chilled bones.

Jake went out, and she dared to look around. It was a beautiful room with floor-length windows looking out on to a terrace and rose garden. Flying trophies by the dozen were lodged in an unobtrusive glass corner cupboard. A whisky decanter and glasses stood on a low polished table by the fire and the bookcases were full. It was a masculine room, but comfortable and well lived in.

'Here, drink this.' Jake came back, carrying a glass.

'What is it?'

'Egg and brandy. It will do you good.'

He grimaced slightly as he saw her suspicious face. 'Don't look like that. There's only a little brandy in it. I'm not trying to make you drunk.'

She sipped it and it went through her veins like fire. After a long silence she said in a small voice, 'Why are you doing all this for me?'

He gave her a long, level look. 'Don't you know?' There was a curious catch in his deep voice.

She shook her head. He turned and strode to the window. Snow was beginning to fall heavily now, covering the terrace and garden with white.

'Why did you leave the flying club?' he asked her abruptly. 'Was it because of Alan?'

'Alan? No. No, not at all!' How could he think that?

Or was he taunting her? Mocking the real reason? Surely her feelings towards him were plain for all to see?

'If it was because of the things I've said, because of what I said to you about the runway, then I hope you'll change your mind.' He was a dark shape, looking away from her, out on to the winter snow. She sipped her drink again.

'I have been unfair to you, Cindy, and I owe you an apology. I realised that the other evening, when you told me about your aunt.'

Unbidden, tears sprang to her eyes. It was the unexpected softness in his tone that stripped away her last defences. Suddenly she was sobbing and shaking as if her heart would break. 'No,' she gulped, 'no. You haven't. Been unfair. You said I was selfish and you were right. You don't know just how right——' She put up a hand to dash at the tears on her cheeks.

Swiftly he came across the room to her.

'Don't be ridiculous,' he said fiercely. She looked up at him piteously. He drew in his breath sharply. For one absurd moment she thought he was going to bend down and take her in his arms, but he only reached out and took the empty glass from her white knuckles. Then he sat down facing her on the long settee.

'Why do you say that?' he asked with quiet insistence. 'Tell me.'

And suddenly it was all pouring out. Her marriage, and how it had gone so wrong. How Simon had come home late that final evening, and how she had told him of her regret in marrying him. The bitterness, and the way that Simon had stormed out. The accident . . .

She omitted nothing, confessing the whole dreadful story for the first time, not hiding her part in the terrible sequence of events. Tears poured down her face and Jake let her cry, sitting very quiet and still, listening, saying nothing.

When she had at last sobbed out the story to its hideous, fatal end, he got up and paced the Persian rug in front of the fire. It was so quiet in the room that she could hear the whispering fall of ashes in the grate. Then Jake seemed to come to a decision. He stopped, turned, and said seriously, 'There's something I think you ought to know about that night, Cindy. It won't be very pleasant for you, I'm afraid. It will come as a shock, I'm sure. But it will complete the picture for you, and I hope, very much, that in time it will help to ease your mind.'

She looked up at him, amazed and fearful, damp channels of tears on her cheeks.

'What is it?' she whispered. 'What can you possibly know about it?'

He looked at her for several seconds, as if measuring her mental strength, and in his look there seemed to be both warmth and compassion.

'Myra knew your husband,' he said finally. 'When I mentioned you to her she recognised the name, and asked me whether your husband had, by any chance, been a designer. She knew Simon because she used to share a flat in London with another actress, a girl called Natalie Hayes.'

'I know that name!' she cut in. 'Simon used to go out with her.'

'Yes. And I'm afraid he carried on going out with her—or rather staying in with her—throughout your marriage. Myra said he was a regular visitor at the flat. Their affair was well known among all Natalie's friends. But Natalie gradually got tired of the whole thing. On the day he died she told him it was over. He stormed out in the early evening, but came back later that night to try and make her change her mind. He sat in the girls' flat drinking whisky until Natalie finally threw him out in the early hours. Apparently he stood outside making all kinds of wild threats. One was to burn down Natalie's country cottage in Wales, and she thinks that might have been where he was heading for when he crashed his car.'

'Oh.' She drew in her breath, taking in the story.

'Poor Simon.' It hurt to know he had been seeing someone else, but after this long time her heart contracted more for her poor, weak husband and his double rejection on the day of his death. She sat very quietly, mulling over the story, a waif-like figure among the deep downy cushions of the settee, her surroundings forgotten.

Jake seemed to sense she needed time alone.

'I'll take your case up,' he said. 'Perhaps later you would do me a favour and phone Sarah. She needs to know that someone has taken you in hand. The telephone's in the hall.'

She could not have said how much later it was that she got up stiffly from where she had been sitting motionless, and went to the telephone alcove in the hall. But by the time she did so, Jake's news had penetrated deeply enough to loosen the iron grip of guilt that had held her for so long.

It did not alter in any way her own part in Simon's tragedy, but it was a help to know that it was not she, and she alone, who had prompted him to take that final, reckless drive. And Sarah's loving greeting fed back still more warmth into her chilled being. Her friend did not seem remotely surprised when she told her where she was staying, but only begged Cindy to forgive her for interfering. 'I was so worried about you, love, and I just didn't know where to turn. I know you of old. I was sure you were neither eating, nor sleeping.'

'No,' she admitted reluctantly, 'I wasn't. But I still don't know why Jake went to all the bother of bringing me here. Although he's got a house full of Christmas guests, so I don't suppose one small extra one makes any difference.'

Even as she spoke, she heard cars draw up outside and saw the front door burst open. Chattering and laughing, Myra and two tall blond men came into the hall, stamping snow from their boots. She shrank back into the alcove. The two men went on upstairs, but Myra ran into the drawing room, calling Jake.

From where she stood listening with only half an ear to Sarah's chatter, Cindy saw Jake come downstairs and follow her into the drawing room. Myra, cheeks glowing from the cold, vibrant in her red flying suit, flung her arms round him. Jake held her slightly away from him so he could hear what she was saying. Cindy could not catch the words, but she could see all too clearly. Myra held out her left hand to him, turning it so the white light from the thickening snow outside caught the huge diamond on her left finger. Jake took up her hand, admiring the effect. Then he hugged her warmly.

Woodenly she finished her conversation with Sarah, put the telephone down and stood staring sightlessly at the wall. Behind her she heard a light step as Myra ran laughing up the stairs, perfectly at home in the elegant manor of which she would soon be mistress.

Jake came out into the hall.

'Cindy, I've put your case in the third room on the left upstairs. I'm sure you'd like to go up and get some rest.' He crooked his mouth at her, almost apologetically. 'I'm afraid I doctored your drink a little—just enough to make sure you get a few hours' sleep today. Judging by those black circles under your eyes, you badly need it. Especially as there will be a bit of a party tonight, and I'd very much like you to be fit enough to join in. There's an engagement to celebrate—and, of course, the first white Christmas for years.'

'I'm not really feeling in a party mood.' It was the understatement of all time, she thought.

'No, I'm sure. But see how you feel after a rest. Shall I show you your room?'

'No. I'll find it.' She turned, anxious only to get away, but certain sleep would not come to ease her troubled mind.

Yet she was asleep almost as soon as she slipped beneath the bedcovers in the room she had been allotted—a deep, sweet sleep that she had not known for years.

When she came swimming up out of it, hours later, it was dark, and someone was drawing across the wine-coloured velvet curtains.

'Cindy,' the shape whispered, 'it's Myra. I'm sorry, I didn't mean to wake you. Jake asked me to look in and see if there was anything you needed.'

She struggled into full consciousness, and as she did so the memory of Myra's engagement hit her like a dull blow.

'No, I'm fine,' she said stiffly. 'Thank you.'

Myra laughed, her happiness bubbling over like a spring, washing aside Cindy's reserve.

'I don't know if Jake's getting lazy these days, or becoming slightly more chivalrous about not barging unasked into ladies' bedrooms. But he despatched me on this errand from the far side of the house—and his room's only next door!'

'Oh.' She smiled weakly. It seemed strange that they even bothered with separate bedrooms, under the circumstances.

There was a pause. Cindy struggled up against the luxurious, sweet-smelling pillows and switched on her bedside light. Myra walked across and perched on the end of the bed. Cindy swallowed. She felt woolly-headed and sleepy-eyed, at a definite disadvantage for whatever conversation was to follow, and to pre-empt what Myra was about to tell her, she said, 'Jake told me about Simon and your friend. I'm glad he did.'

Myra grimaced. 'Natalie was no friend of mine. We just happened to need a flat at about the same time.'

'Oh.'

There was an awkward pause. She allowed her gaze to drop to the enormous diamond on Myra's slender finger.

'Congratulations—on your engagement. I mean.'

Myra looked at the ring and laughed. Her eyes showed that she was brimming with joy. 'Sometimes I think I must be crazy,' she said, 'marrying a flyer. You know what they're like, from the club. It's aeroplanes first and aeroplanes last, and a wife comes trailing somewhere far behind. Still, it's my choice so I'm sure I'll find a way of living with it—somehow!'

She stood up. 'You're sure I can't get you anything? You've got your own bathroom, through that door there.' She indicated vaguely. 'But I'm sure you know that. Drinks are in the drawing room, at seven.'

'Are there many people staying here?' She certainly couldn't cope with a large gathering of strangers.

'No, only four besides myself and Jake. There's a man called Steve Windward and his wife. They're Canadians. And Mike, who's American, and you. Don't worry, everyone's really friendly.'

She sank back in the bed as Myra went out. Suddenly it was perfectly plain why she was here. Jake had odd numbers for his Christmas house party! Rescuing her from festive loneliness at Rose Cottage had tied in perfectly with his own arrangements!

Sick of heart, she climbed out of bed and put on her satin robe. She ran her hands through her curls, freeing them from tangles, as she walked across to the bathroom. But the door opened not on to the expected tiles and porcelain, but into a decidedly masculine bedroom, with a shaggy white fur thrown across the enormous bed. Jake stood in front of an open wardrobe, clad only in a brief towel which was startlingly white against his tanned skin.

She gasped, rooted to the spot. Jake regarded her with interest, the old familiar taunting light kindling in his eyes as he took in her presence.

'I'm sorry. I thought this was the bathroom,' she stammered out, blushing deeply.

He came over to her. 'What a pity,' he observed, his mouth quirking. 'For a moment I thought the tables had turned, and it was your turn to force your attentions on me!'

He was taunting her, as he had done so often before. Yet, unlike on previous occasions, he also seemed to be inviting her to laugh with him, sharing the joke.

Perhaps he felt sorry for her, after telling her the bad news about Simon and Natalie? Or perhaps his engagement to Myra had robbed him of the need to subject and conquer?

But then the smile faded, and he was looking down at her with a deep, dark, unfathomable gaze. For a second she was sure he was going to draw her to him. She felt the certainty like a prickle on her skin and her hands moved involuntarily, although whether to embrace him or push him away, she could not be sure.

Instead, though, he turned abruptly.

'Did you sleep?'

'Yes.'

'Good. Your bathroom is the other door. I hope you can join us downstairs at seven.'

Dismissed, she backed clumsily out of his room and sought the sanctuary of her bathroom. The encounter had left her trembling and unnerved, and it was only with the greatest effort that she began to think herself into a suitable frame of mind for the evening. It would be torture, but she would survive it, as she had survived so many things already in her short life. Somehow, from somewhere, she would find the good grace to wish Jake and Myra well. After all, she liked Myra and knew she would be a good match for Jake.

As if summoning extra courage, she dressed with meticulous care for the evening ahead. She brushed out her hair till it shone and hid her pallor with subtle blusher. She looked better than she had managed to do for weeks, and that knowledge cheered her the tiniest fraction as she made her way reluctantly downstairs.

She was late. She had heard Jake's door close and his firm footsteps go down the panelled corridor outside her room a good fifteen minutes before. Even so, she had lingered in front of her mirror, fiddling nervously with her hair and dress, dreading the moment when she would have to don her mask of party gaiety.

So as she stepped down the wide oak stairs, she could hear the celebrations already underway. She paused in the hall. Corks popped and then there was a toast. The voice was muffled by the almost-closed door, but she heard quite plainly the end of it, the invitation to drink to 'Jake and Myra'.

'Jake and Myra,' chorused voices, then there was a general hub-bub of laughter and good cheer. She took a huge breath, pushed open the door and arrived just in time to see Jake bending his head to kiss Myra as they stood together on the richly patterned rug by the fire. There was a roaring in her ears as she realised that here, at last, was a test for which she lacked the strength. Her knees sagged and she clutched the brass doorknob. She had to lower her head in order not to faint.

Luckily no one had seen her tentative entrance. She took another deep breath, to stop the spinning whiteness before her eyes, then raised her head. Jake was looking across at her. Heart hammering, she turned abruptly and fled headlong, not caring where she was going, turning down passages and opening doors in frantic urge to escape.

If only she could just get out of the house! Then she would be free. She could make her way back to Rose Cottage, her lonely haven, lock all the doors, and hide herself completely from the world and all the cruel troubles it brought!

Somehow she found herself in the kitchen. On winged feet she ran the length of the huge, stone-flagged room and tugged open the heavy back door.

Then she was outside, in the cold air, among whirling snowflakes. Instantly her strappy sandals sank into a small drift of snow.

'Oh!' Madly, she tore them off and ran forward on bare feet. The searing cold was almost welcome after the red hotness of choking jealousy and shame.

'Cindy!'

Jake was coming after her. She mustn't let him catch up with her! He would only chastise her, yet again, for her spoilt selfishness, her foolishness.

She ran faster, round the side of the manor house.

Suddenly she was on the terrace outside the drawing room. Windows spilled a yellow glow of light on to the snow, and through them she could see figures clustered round the fire. She shrank back. Jake caught her, his hands on her bare shoulders, and whirled her round to face him.

'What the hell do you think you're doing?'

'Leave me alone, Jake Seaton! Why can't you leave me alone? I should never have let you bring me here.' Her voice was wild with uncontrollable sobs.

'Leave you alone?' he said harshly. 'I wish I could. That's what I've been trying to do all this time.' His eyes went over her, angry and demanding, then his lips were coming down, taking hers, savage, relentless. Her legs buckled against him. His kiss sent a huge spreading warmth inside her and her heart seemed to swell as if it would explode.

Yet she fought to turn her head from him, gasping against his dark jacket, 'What are you doing——? You mustn't——'

His hands were tangling in her hair, forcing her head round to him again. 'I've tried to leave you alone ever since that first evening, but I couldn't. I just couldn't.'

His lips were finding hers again, punishingly sweet and forbidden.

'Don't,' she sobbed. 'Don't. Why do you always treat me like this? Someone will see—Myra——'

He pulled back from her, his dark eyes questioning.

'Myra?'

'Yes, Myra!' she spat out savagely. He seemed determined to mock her. 'Myra. Your fiancée. The woman you got engaged to today. Don't you remember? Or doesn't it matter to you? You seem to think you can behave exactly as you like——'

A range of expressions passed over his face, puzzlement, then a clearing of his brow. He laughed, throwing his head back. Her fists closed in fury against his chest, ready to fight her way backwards out of his tormenting, heady embrace. But he was turning her round in his arms, pointing.

'Look,' he said against her ear, as he had once done when pointing out the airfield from her cottage window, on their first fateful meeting. Inside the lighted room, like players on a stage, Myra leaned contentedly on the arm of a rangy blond man. 'Myra got engaged to my friend Mike Peel today. He's the man you saw flying the Pitts earlier today.'

'Oh!' Her lips parted in astonishment. 'Myra and *Mike*! I thought the toast was to Myra and *Jake*!' Then she remembered. 'But when I came into the room, I saw the two of you together. You were kissing her——'

He turned her back in his arms to face him. 'In congratulations—as her host and an old friend.'

'You mean you and she were never—— And all this time I thought—— Especially that morning at the flying club——'

'When she had just telephoned Mike in America to ask him over for Christmas!' Jake grinned, a little apologetically. 'I could see what was in the wind between the two of them, and thought an English country Christmas might do the trick. But I could also see what was going through your mind that morning and must admit I wasn't entirely adverse to your misreading the situation. I was so angry with you about the runway—and other things. I suppose I hoped you might feel a twinge of jealousy.'

'A twinge! But you seemed so well-matched——'

His grin faded.

'Look, you might as well know the full truth, before the village gossips get to you. Myra and I did have a brief affair—and I mean brief—when she first came up here to learn to fly. We both quickly realised we made better friends than lovers, but that's not to say we didn't enjoy each other's company. I was on my own, and Mike was away in America, so there was no reason for us not to go around together. She's always stayed here when she's come up for her flying lessons, and I've been glad to have the house filled and used. It's far too big for one——' He searched her face.

'Did it matter to you?' he asked. 'What you thought about Myra?'

'Yes,' she admitted reluctantly. She forced herself to meet his gaze. It was too late to pretend. His arms tightened about her. Now he would be able to take what he wanted. Her. His revenge.

'Oh, Cindy, my dearest love!'

His kiss was sweet, lingering, entirely without savagery or contempt. It melted her utterly, so that she yearned against him, wanting to lose herself in his arms. Unnoticed the snow settled on their entwined shoulders and arms. Something clattered on to the stone flags. With lingering reluctance, Jake drew his lips from hers.

'Oh, Cindy!' There was something almost like a break in his voice. 'You utter idiot. What on earth are you doing barefoot in the snow?'

'I couldn't run in my shoes. I took them off.'

'You ridiculous girl! It's high time someone took you in hand.'

Instinctively she stiffened in his arms, a distant echo of chill fear seeping through her newly flowering happiness.

'What do you mean?'

He drew her back close to him. 'I want you here, with me. As my wife. But it wouldn't be like before, I promise you. I fell in love with you because of your independence, your spirit. I won't trap you, or tie you down. I won't stop you painting. I'll *make* you paint. In fact I'll be your first customer—I want to buy that picture of the Pitts I saw in your cottage the other evening. It's the most marvellous painting of an aeroplane I've ever seen.'

She closed her eyes and leaned close to him. It seemed such happiness was impossible. 'Buy it,' she said, 'never! It's a present. I was painting it for you all the time, although I wouldn't ever admit it to myself.'

'Is that an acceptance? Does that mean you forgive me for how badly I've treated you? I didn't want to fall in love with the woman who was denying me the very thing I needed most. That's why I had to convince myself how selfishly thoughtless you were. But you were invading my thoughts from that very first moment! When I made you come up to the airfield that first time I knew you wouldn't change your mind about the runway. It was just an excuse, a way of seeing you again. Then when I saw you going around with that young fool Jenkins——' He broke off, looking down at her. 'But I had no right to treat you as I did——' he said softly.

'Forgive? I'm the one who should be asking that—That first night—I should never——'

He pulled her closer. 'That's enough about that. We both behaved—well, precipitously. Perhaps we were both ahead of ourselves. It isn't important. Although——' He held her back from him and she could see both humour and passion mingling in his dark gaze. 'I'm not sure I could stand it twice.'

In answer she reached to draw him closer again. 'It won't happen again,' she whispered 'Not tonight, not any night. Not ever again.'

SPECIAL FREE OFFER

Janet Dailey

TREASURY EDITION

- *NO QUARTER ASKED*
- *FIESTA SAN ANTONIO*
- *FOR BITTER OR WORSE*

Now's your chance to rediscover your favorite Janet Dailey romance characters – Cord and Stacey Harris, and Travis McCrea.

Own three Janet Dailey novels in one deluxe hardcover edition. A beautifully bound volume in gold-embossed leatherette...an attractive addition to any home library.

Here's how to get this special offer from Harlequin! As simple as 1...2...3!

DECEMBER
TREASURY EDITION
COUPON

1. Each month, save one Treasury Edition coupon from your favorite Romance or Presents novel.
2. In four months you'll have saved four Treasury Edition coupons (<u>only one coupon per month allowed</u>).
3. Then all you have to do is fill out and return the order form provided, along with the four Treasury Edition coupons required and $1.00 for postage and handling.

Mail to: Harlequin Reader Service

In the U.S.A.
2504 West Southern Ave.
Tempe, AZ 85282

In Canada
P.O. Box 2800, Postal Station A
5170 Yonge Street
Willowdale, Ont. M2N 6J3

RT1-E-2

Please send me my FREE copy of the Janet Dailey Treasury Edition. I have enclosed the four Treasury Edition coupons required and $1.00 for postage and handling along with this order form.

(Please Print)

NAME_____

ADDRESS_____

CITY_____

STATE/PROV._____ ZIP/POSTAL CODE_____

SIGNATURE_____
This offer is limited to one order per household.

SUPPLIES LIMITED

This special Janet Dailey offer expires January 1986.

Take 4 best-selling love stories FREE
Plus get a FREE surprise gift!

Special Limited-Time Offer

Mail to   **Harlequin Reader Service®**

In the U.S.
2504 West Southern Ave.
Tempe, AZ 85282

In Canada
P.O. Box 2800, Station "A"
5170 Yonge Street
Willowdale, Ontario M2N 6J3

YES! Please send me 4 free Harlequin Romance® novels and my free surprise gift. Then send me 6 brand-new novels every month as they come off the presses. Bill me at the low price of $1.65 each ($1.75 in Canada)—a 11% saving off the retail price. There are no shipping, handling or other hidden costs. There is no minimum number of books I must purchase. I can always return a shipment and cancel at any time. Even if I never buy another book from Harlequin, the 4 free novels and the surprise gift are mine to keep forever.

Name   (PLEASE PRINT)

Address   Apt. No.

City   State/Prov.   Zip/Postal Code

This offer is limited to one order per household and not valid to present subscribers. Price is subject to change.

HR--SUB--1